The Nahtahn Cartel
THE INC.

B. Love

Prolific Pen Pusher

Preface

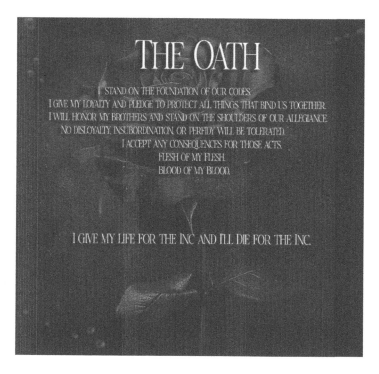

THE OATH

I STAND ON THE FOUNDATION OF OUR CODES.
I GIVE MY LOYALTY AND PLEDGE TO PROTECT ALL THINGS THAT BIND US TOGETHER.
I WILL HONOR MY BROTHERS AND STAND ON THE SHOULDERS OF OUR ALLEGIANCE.
NO DISLOYALTY, INSUBORDINATION, OR PERFIDY WILL BE TOLERATED.
I ACCEPT ANY CONSEQUENCES FOR THOSE ACTS.
FLESH OF MY FLESH.
BLOOD OF MY BLOOD.

I GIVE MY LIFE FOR THE INC AND I'LL DIE FOR THE INC.

For character visuals: https://youtu.be/mbEBDm1pyKE

The Past

1

Gambino Nahtahn

Ashes.

That one word was all it took.

As one of three enforcers for his father, Samson Nahtahn, it was Gambino's responsibility to handle any threats to Samson and the family. When his father gave an order, Gambino never refused.

He never asked questions.

Ashes.

That one word ended Peter's life and was the reason he would burn until his flesh and bones resembled the gray, fiery ashes that fell from Gambino's weed filled cigarillo. Gambino didn't know what Peter had done to deserve death, but he trusted his father's instincts and was confident the punishment was one that was worth it.

After taking one last pull from the blunt, Gambino

flicked it out of the window then headed across the parking lot to the hotel. It was risky meeting with Valerie while her husband was in the city, but Gambino didn't care. Taking a life always filled him with a euphoric high that only busting a nut could pull him down from. And since he'd started sleeping with the older woman six months ago, she'd become a welcomed addiction.

There was something about the thrill of knowing she belonged to another man that excited Gambino. Knowing they shared a secret that would put *both* of their lives on the line if her husband ever found out made their rendezvous that much sweeter. Gambino kept his head down as he made his way through the lobby. Valerie had already sent the suite information—room 3223.

His heartbeat mellowed as he made his way up the elevator, but it raced when she opened the door naked. Gripping her wide hips, Gambino picked her up and wrapped her legs around him. He allowed the door to shut on its own as he carried her to the bed. After tossing her onto it, he stepped back and admired her beauty before unbuckling his jeans.

"Get over here," he commanded with a tilt of his head. "Suck my dick."

A low purr escaped Valerie as she crawled over to him. She took his shaft into her mouth and held the base. His head flung back and eyes focused on the ceiling as he swallowed back a moan.

So warm.

So wet.

So ready.

When Valerie cupped his balls, he groaned and looked down at her. Gambino's hand gripped her hair as he circled his hips and fucked her mouth.

"Argh!" he yelled as she bit down on his dick. He pushed her away as the suite door was kicked off the hinges. With his pants at his ankles, Gambino shuffled backward in his attempt to grab his piece.

It didn't matter.

Six guns were trained on him, by six lethal shooters, and he knew regardless of the shots he let off that he'd die in that room.

The men parted like the Red Sea and Cory made his way through. His eyes shifted from his naked wife as she shook like a leaf in the center of the bed to Gambino as he pulled his boxers and jeans up. Cory's eyes were locked on Gambino's, and in that moment, for the first time, Gambino truly considered the consequences of his actions. They weren't *just* risking his life. They were risking his reputation and respect. For a man like Gambino, those things were supposed to matter most.

Cory was like a second father to Gambino. He was his father's second in command and his consigliere. Gambino loved the influence of the consigliere. While his father was the don, a lot of his decisions were made based on what Cory said. To Gambino, the consigliere was the true boss of all bosses... and that was why he wanted to be one. It was a true honor when Cory agreed to be his mentor. It upset his father for a while, but after hearing Gambino's reasoning, Samson understood and gave his blessing.

It had never been Gambino's intention to sleep with Cory's new wife, but one drunk night at the underground casino led to just that, and Gambino hadn't been able to stop himself from going back to Valerie every time she called.

Cory's steps were calculated as he walked over to the bed. He pulled Valerie to the side of it by her head. She yelped, and though Gambino wanted to step in, he didn't. Effortlessly, Cory pulled his blade and sliced her throat. He held her up as her blood drained, not allowing her body to drop onto the bed until it was lifeless. After cleaning off his blade, Cory slid it back in its sheath that rested against his back.

Gambino's head tilted and heart slowed down as Cory walked in his direction. Regardless of the sin committed, he'd lay down for no man, and he wouldn't be an easy kill. A shaky breath escaped Cory as he crossed his arms over his chest.

"I'm so disappointed in you." His words, his glossy eyes, they were too much for Gambino, so he looked away. "Look at me!" Cory roared, pounding his chest. "You were man enough to fuck my wife, young blood. Don't cower now." He released a bark of laughter before wiping his mouth of the saliva that flew out. Cory waited until Gambino looked at him to say, "My loyalty to your father is the only reason I'm going to let you live. But if you *ever* disrespect me like this again, I will go after everyone you love and save you for last. You don't deserve to be my mentee, and you for damn sure don't deserve the Nahtahn name." Cory spit at his feet, and Gambino gritted his teeth. "Stay the fuck away from me, Bino. You understand me?"

Gambino's head bobbed once as his nostrils flared.

Cory looked over at his wife. "Get a crew in here to clean this shit up, and since you're responsible for her death, you pay for and take care of the funeral."

There was no reason for Gambino to vocally agree because that was exactly what he was going to do. Even if Cory hadn't told him to, his father was going to.

His father.

How was Samson going to react when he heard the news?

There were only a few rules Samson had given his three sons to live by... and never sleeping with a mafia member's wife was at the top of that list. Gambino didn't expect Cory to keep this between them, even if it meant ensuring no shame fell upon him because of his wife's treacherous deeds. Gambino would have to cross or burn that bridge when he got to it. For now, he had to take care of the lifeless woman in bed.

2

G ambino
      Eight Years Later
      New Year's Eve
The Monster's Ball

GAMBINO'S EYES SHIFTED ACROSS THE ROOM. HE ONLY
half listened to what the elder was saying. His focus would

remain shattered until he saw both of his brothers and knew they were okay. They were at the Monster's Ball, and though it was a time of networking and celebration, Gambino was still on high alert. He was always on high alert when so many killers were in the same room.

His eyes settled on Luciano, and Gambino's body relaxed. As the oldest of the three, Gambino took his role as protector seriously. It was his responsibility to make sure his brothers were always okay. His parents expected that from him. Demanded that of him. And the thirty-year-old was committed to making sure he *always* came through.

As if Luciano felt eyes on him, he looked around until he spotted Gambino. They spoke with their eyes and expressions briefly before Gambino looked for Gotti. At twenty-eight and twenty-six, Luciano and Gotti had similarities, but their values and priorities were like night and day. They protected each other fiercely, but the middle and younger brothers were often combative toward each other.

Clearing his throat, Gambino looked down at Antonio. He wasn't a short man, but Gambino was large—in stature, in aura, and in reputation.

"Excuse me, OG. I need to find my brother."

"Handle your business."

While Gambino searched the left side of the room, Luciano took the right. They met in the middle.

"He has to be outside or in the bathroom," Gambino said.

"I wouldn't be surprised if he was fucking somebody."

That was what Gambino feared. Though he'd matured with time, made amends for his horrible choices, and learned the power of discipline, Gambino couldn't say the same for his youngest brother. Gotti was going down a destructive path with his reckless choices, and though

Gambino was all too familiar with that way of living, he wanted better for his brother. As they walked toward the bathrooms, Gambino casually grabbed a flute of champagne from a server they passed. He gulped it down, wiped his mouth, then set it on the closest table.

The door of the women's bathroom opened, and a woman stepped out with a wide smile. She ran her hands down her dress and fluffed her hair before heading in their direction. Seconds later, Gotti opened the same door and came out. He wiped his forehead with one hand and straightened his bowtie with the other. A long sigh escaped Gambino as his brother walked over to them with a grin. He rubbed his palms together as he closed the space between them.

"Who was that?" Luciano asked.

With a shrug, Gotti looked in the direction the woman had gone. "I think she said her name was Moné. I'on know."

"Is her man here?" Gambino asked. "She has to be attached to a family in this room. You playing a dangerous game, brotha."

Sucking his teeth, Gotti waved his hand dismissively. "I'on really give a fuck about allat. We showed our faces, I came, now we can go."

"Which one of 'em." Gambino turned toward the sound of the question. "Which one of these motherfuckers were you in the bathroom with?"

The woman's eyes locked on Gotti, but she didn't respond. A snivel escaped her as he tightened his grip on her arm. As much as Gambino didn't want to get involved, he also didn't want his brother to be the reason the ball took a violent turn.

"Why don't you let her go, and we can talk about this outside?" Gambino suggested.

"So it was you?"

He tossed her to the side, but she regrouped quickly. Tugging at his suit jacket, she pleaded with him to leave. However, the middle aged man paid her no attention as his eyes shifted from one brother to the next.

"It was me," Gotti said. "Wassup?"

"You fucked my wife?"

"Yeah, and based on how tight and wet that pussy was, I might do it again."

Regardless of how Gambino felt about Gotti's actions, he'd always defend him publicly. Gambino unbuttoned his tuxedo jacket and rested his hand on his Glock. He'd never been the type to go back and forth with a man and wouldn't start now. The moment he was tired of the exchange or sensed the man would make a move, he'd shoot. Luciano had taken the same stance, and they huddled around Gotti as he listened to the man yell.

Gambino knew all hell was about to break loose when Gotti smiled and bobbed his head. He was the only person Gambino knew who loved fighting and got so much joy out of it that he smiled the whole time. Resting his hand on Gotti's chest, Gambino almost whispered, "This is not the place for this. We're here to represent Pops. Walk away."

Gotti's teeth gritted as he considered his brother's words. Only a few seconds passed before his stance softened and he took a few steps back. He walked away, and Luciano followed. Gambino waited until they both were out safely to turn and leave. They were already in the SUV, so he hopped in and loosened his tie.

"This is why I don't be wanting to go anywhere with you," Luciano scolded. "We can't take your ass *nowhere*."

Sucking his teeth, Gotti pulled his phone out of his

pocket and ignored his brother's words. His brows wrinkled as he sat up straight in his seat. "Mommy called y'all?"

Gambino's head shook as he pulled out his phone. "She knows we're at the ball, so she shouldn't be calling."

"Something is wrong," Luciano said, lifting his phone to his ear.

"She called me too," Gambino replied. As Luciano listened to the voicemail she'd left, Gambino called her back. She answered almost instantly, and the sound of her sniffles made his heart drop. "Ma? What's wrong?"

"You boys need to get back home."

"Okay, but what's wrong?"

Her breath was shaky. "It's your father. He's in the hospital."

2:00 AM

GAMBINO TOOK LONG STRIDES DOWN THE HALL. His brothers followed closely behind. Running his fingers down the corners of his mouth, he said a silent prayer. When he talked to his mother hours ago, all she could tell him was that Samson had collapsed. The hours it took for them to get from Miami to Rose Valley Hills were excruciating as he wondered what happened to his father and if he would be okay.

Thankfully, Cory hadn't told Samson about Valerie and Gambino. The punishment of not having Cory's guidance and respect was enough. No amount of amends restored that relationship, and it was one of Gambino's biggest regrets. The other? Cheating on the woman he was sure he'd marry with Valerie. He'd lost both of them eight years ago, and neither lost had been filled yet.

"Mommy, we here," Gotti said before disconnecting the call.

Not long after, Claire came rushing out of the room. Her eyes leaked. Her hair and loose fitted clothes moved fluidly as she all but jogged over to them. It didn't surprise Gambino when Gotti gently pushed him out of the way to get to her. He was a mama's boy while Gambino was closest to their father. Luciano, like a true middle child, held the same detached but loving relationship with both parents.

Claire collapsed in Gotti's arms as she looked from Gambino to Luciano.

"He's gone, my babies. H-he had a heart attack, and he's gone."

It appeared all her strength left as she confessed those words. Gotti slid down onto the floor with her and held her as she cried. Luciano gripped her shoulder, gaze distant as he stared toward the room she'd come out of. The room where his father's spirit had left him. Short steps led Gambino in its direction.

When he walked in and saw his father's lifeless body on the bed, it nearly knocked the wind out of him. Heat radiated through his body as he hovered over Samson. His hand rested on his father's chest. The lack of movement was foreign. Unreal. Tears instantly prickled his eyes, but when he felt his mother's arms wrap around him, he sniffled and quickly dried them.

Gambino refused to show weakness—not even in front of his mother.

"The arrangements were already made," Claire said, squeezing his arms. "You are the don now. Samson prepared you for this moment. Are you ready?"

Was he ready?

His father hadn't been gone for a whole day. He hadn't been able to grieve yet. Unfortunately, this was their life. Regardless of if he was ready or not, it was time for Gambino to take over. He'd always wanted to be consigliere not the don. Not the boss of all bosses. Not the face of the Nahtahn Cartel. Gripping the bed, Gambino hung his head as he released a hard breath.

"Yeah, I'm ready."

"Good. The celebration of life begins tomorrow. Let your brothers know whatever you need."

When she tried to walk away, Gambino turned and gently gripped her hand. He pulled her into his chest, and she clung to his back.

"I'm here."

Those two words released another dam of tears. He held his mother close as she cried. For some reason, it gave him strength to believe she was crying for them both.

3

K ayla
  Five Days Later

KAYLA PREFERRED TO BE ANYWHERE BUT IN THE TOWN car heading to Samson Nahtahn's funeral with her father. Kayla had no problems with Samson while he was living. At one point, she thought he'd be her father-in-law. Eight years ago, Gambino's cheating changed that. Worse, he broke up with her before she could leave him. Her mother convinced her the best revenge was moving on and being loved properly, but Kayla prayed every day, for quite some time, that he actually suffered.

Regardless of how Gambino's actions hurt her all those years ago, a part of her hated that his father was gone. The loss of a parent was a punishment she wouldn't wish on her worst enemy. Even with that empathy and compassion, Kayla didn't want to see Gambino, and she hoped he

13

wouldn't see her in the sea of people that she was sure would be at the funeral.

Since Samson's death, an event had been held in his honor every day. Her father had attended three, but this was the first time she would be paying her respects. Her heart beat wildly against her chest as they pulled up to the church. She hadn't seen Gambino in a while, and the last thing she wanted was for residual hurt and anger to rise to the surface today.

Regardless of how death lingered within their lifestyle, there was always an underlying grief that many of the members of the family opted out of handling in a healthy manner. Some turned to more violence and drugs, others sex... Kayla wondered what Gambino's vice would be. Last she heard, he was a changed man. Her bitterness wouldn't allow her to be happy about his growth.

"I know things didn't end well with you and Bino," her father, Bernie, said.

Kayla scoffed as she stared at the church as people filed in. "That's putting it mildly."

Bernie rested his hand on her thigh. "Look at me, honey."

Slowly, her head turned in her father's direction. "Yes, Papa?"

"I appreciate you coming with me to show respect, especially since your mom was too sick to join us. Today isn't about you and Gambino. It's about celebrating Samson's life. Remember that."

Kayla nodded her agreement. In his subtle way, Bernie told her not to make the day about herself. Her anger and hurt had no space in that church. So as difficult as it may be, she vowed not to let her emotions get the best of her.

"Yes, sir."

After the chauffeur came to a stop, he opened Bernie's door, then Kayla's. As she wrapped her fur around her chest, Kayla pulled in a deep breath. Arms linked, they walked inside the church. Its burgundy and gold décor combined with the massive space and high ceilings gave the church an old school vibe. It didn't surprise Kayla when her father went down to the front of the church, sliding into a pew that was behind where Samson's family would be seated.

Samson's family.

They stood in front of his casket. All three of his sons wore dark shades over their eyes. Claire's low sitting hat and handkerchief covered her face, but Kayla could tell by her shuddering shoulders that she was crying. Sniffling, Kayla pulled in a deep breath to dry her own tears so they wouldn't fall.

Samson was like a second father to her. Even after the break up, he treated her like the daughter he always wanted. He bought her things, lent his ear and mind for advice, and met her for lunch twice a month. Kayla was sure her relationship with Gambino's family would be over when they broke up, but she was glad that hadn't been the case.

As the Nahtahn family walked to the front pew, Kayla held her breath, hoping Gambino wouldn't notice her. She wasn't surprised when his eyes began to scan the room. Regardless of the situation, he was always on alert. When his eyes landed on her, Kayla's heart stopped beating. She swallowed hard and tried to convince herself he wasn't looking at her.

Gambino lowered his shades, and his piercing coffee brown eyes stared right at her.

Swallowing hard, she ran her hand down her neck and

looked away. Her mind instantly took her to the last time she talked to Gambino—eight years ago, right after Valerie's funeral.

He hovered over the casket, as if he was her husband... not Cory. Afterward, he was a drunken mess. It didn't take her long to figure out what the problem was, but her suspicions were confirmed when she walked in on Gambino swiping through pictures of him and Valerie as a single tear slid down his cheek. In his drunken state, he confessed to his guilt more than grief. He was hurt more than he was sad. Hurt that he allowed his flesh to rule, costing Valerie her life and his relationship with Cory.

Before Kayla could stop herself, she smacked the side of his face.

"You fucked her!" she roared as he leaped from his seat. It was as if he hadn't paid attention to who he was confessing to. Or maybe he didn't care.

"Kayla, I—"

"No! I don't want to hear your excuses. I can't believe you cheated on me!"

Another quick slap to his face caused Gambino to grab her out of reflex, but she shimmied out of his hold.

"Now ain't the time for this. I'm grieving and drunk. I'm not about to go back and forth with your ass."

"You're grieving?" Kayla chuckled as she clutched her chest. "Oh, excuse me. I'm sorry for being upset while you grieve the bitch you cheated on me with."

Gambino's expression hardened as he pointed toward her. "Watch your mouth, Kayla."

Their eyes remained locked as hers leaked. When the weight of the moment settled within Kayla, she ran her fingers through her wavy hair and took a step back.

"Did you love her?"

He stumbled slightly before turning and grabbing his bottle of whisky. "No, but that's not the point."

"Then what's the point, Gambino?"

"The point is, you're not built for this life. A good wife wouldn't be in here questioning me right now, and she for damn sure wouldn't be so weak that she'd put her feelings on me while I'm struggling to process my own. You have no couth, no decorum, and I don't know what the fuck I was thinking agreeing to even marry you. We're over."

Kayla's tongue ran over her teeth before she released a low, shaky chuckle. "You stand here, having buried your mistress, and you speak to me about couth and decorum? Fuck you!"

"Nah, fuck you!"

It was in that moment, when Gambino closed the space between them, that Kayla realized she was looking at and talking to a stranger. He'd been drinking so much she smelled it seeping from his pores. His eyes were red, puffy, and dark. Lifeless. He didn't look like himself. The disheveled look of his hair grown out was the complete opposite of the man she'd fallen in love with.

Regardless of that truth, Kayla had never been the kind of woman to accept disrespect. Not when her father was a man who'd killed people for doing it. Gritting her teeth, Kayla nodded and took a step back.

"When you come out of your grief and drunkenness, you're going to realize the horrible mistake you just made."

"The only mistake I made was being with you."

Before Kayla could stop herself, her hand reared back to smack him again. That time, Gambino was prepared. H grabbed her arm and pulled it behind her back. Pulling her forcefully into his chest, he lowered his lips to hers and kissed her. With all her might, she pushed him away before stum-

bling out of his room. Her back rested against the wall as she pulled in ragged breaths. After wiping steadily falling tears, Kayla looked back at the door and vowed she'd never be alone with the man she loved again.

The feel of her father's hand on her back pulled Kayla out of her flashback. "Are you okay?"

Nodding, Kayla forced a smile. "I'm fi—"

"Kitten."

Her eyes snapped shut at the sound of the nickname Gambino had given her years ago. He called her that because of the light green color of her eyes. He said they reminded him of the kitten his mother had when he was a child. The way Gambino used to look into her eyes, it was like he was staring into the deepest pit of her soul.

"Can we talk?" Gambino asked with a softness, a carefulness in his tone that wasn't there the last time they'd spoken.

Bernie searched her eyes as they watered. "You don't have to if you don't want to," he assured her.

"It's fine, Papa."

When she felt emotionally composed, Kayla stood and exited the row she was seated on. She didn't bother looking at Gambino. The second his hand tried to rest on the small of her back, Kayla casually put space between them. They stepped into the cream colored hall to the left of the sanctuary. Leaning against the wall for support, Kayla continued to avoid his eyes. She didn't realize she was tugging her fingers and twiddling her thumbs until his large hand covered hers. Instantly, the nervous fidgeting stopped.

"You don't have to be nervous," Gambino said softly. Pulling her hands away from his, Kayla pulled them behind her back. "You can't look at me, kitten?"

Licking the corner of her mouth, Kayla shook her head.

She vowed to not cause a scene, so it was best that way. For eight years, they uttered no words to one another. There were times she was forced to be in the same room as Gambino, but she never looked at him. Never allowed him to get this close.

"What do you want?" she asked quietly.

"I wanted to apologize." That made Kayla snap her eyes in his direction. "I was fucked up." He smiled, but his eyes watered slightly. His eyes—they were light, vibrant, and full of life. That was different. "I was operating in my ego. My pride. I was thoughtless and heartless. I tried to love you, but I didn't really know how. That version of me... you didn't deserve that." A frown covered her face. How was she supposed to still hate him with him saying things like that? "I just... Pops loved you. You were his daughter, and he reminded me every day after we broke up that I was dumb as hell and didn't deserve you." That made them both smile. "One day about two years ago, he finally told me he was proud of the man I'd become. Said all that to say, thank you for coming. Not for me but for him. And I really am sorry about how things ended between us."

Gambino placed a kiss to the center of her head that made her gasp as chills covered her arms and her nipples hardened. She watched as he walked back into the sanctuary, suddenly unable to keep her eyes off him.

4

G ambino

EVERY TIME HIS EYES CLOSED, HE SAW HER. KAYLA Lattimore was a twenty-nine year old *stallion*. She was tall and curvy with a round, natural ass. Her skin was the color of cashews without a tattoo or blemish in sight. Light green eyes held Gambino captive many nights years ago. Her hair, stopping at her plump ass, was wavy in pattern and often worn down. To Gambino, Kayla was absolutely perfect, and he hated that she was the one who got away.

With time and therapy, Gambino realized he pushed her away because he knew he didn't deserve her. She was a good woman and good lover, and the better she treated him when he was at his lowest, the worse it made him feel. The things he said to her the day of Valerie's funeral weren't true. In his drunken state, he tried to say anything he could to hurt her and get her to walk away. Now, he wished he would have had the courage to be honest with her. The courage to tell her he didn't feel worthy of her and hoped she'd give him the time and grace to become a better version of himself. The version of himself that he was now.

"Where your head at?" Gambino looked up at the sound of Luciano's voice.

The brothers were at their parents' home for a large dinner. Though it was hosted by the other four families in the commission, Claire requested to do it in the comfort of the home she shared with Samson. All heads of the five families plus their cartel leaders were in attendance.

After they discussed business and the fact that Gambino would have to be officially sworn in and recite the oath, they had dinner. Now, Gambino was in his father's study reflecting and hoping his father's spirit would meet him there. As his brothers sat at the round table with him, Gambino figured Samson urged them to find him in his stead.

Gambino wanted to tell Luciano that his head was with his heart, and both were with Kayla. Deciding not to answer, he shifted the conversation toward something he needed to speak with them about anyway.

"We can't wait until the grand meeting with the commission in March. I have to be sworn in now," Gambino told them.

The grand meeting was a meeting held every March for the commission. During that time, the leaders of every cartel paid their 10 percent dues, and new members were sworn into THE INC. THE INC was a mafia cartel started by Julio Hundero. He ran one of the largest cartels from Cuba, but knew times were changing, and came to the USA for a change.

Newer cartels rose while Julio fell, unable to catch up

with the innovative changes. He used his position as the president of the Zulu fraternity at Howard University, which was already into illegal dealings, to elevate himself and his son Juan. For Juan, the fraternity wasn't just a brotherhood. It was the foundation for his new empire. His new cartel. It was the perfect mix of old school principles and new school strategies.

Operating under the radar, they expanded into new markets, leveraging their education, connections, and tech-savvy ways to push product faster, cleaner, and with a reach that stretched further than Julio could have ever imagined.

Gambino's grandfather, Rufus Nahtahn, was one of the founding members of THE INC with Juan. After his death, Samson took over. Now, it was Gambino's turn.

"Naturally," Luciano said, cutting his cigar. "When will this happen?"

"And what do you need from us?" Gotti added.

"I'll be sworn in as the official don and boss of all bosses for the Nahtahn Cartel after Pops celebration is over, so in three days. As far as what I need from the two of you..." Gambino paused and looked at one brother then the other. "With my position changing, so will both of yours."

"Gotti, you'll remain capo, but I want you over the legal businesses. You've been moving reckless lately and the last thing I need is for your words and actions to start a war during this new transition."

Around Thanksgiving, Gotti was involved in a shootout in broad fucking daylight. The only reason he wasn't in prison now was because of how many officers were on their payroll. While their power and money may have kept them out of prison, it didn't change the commission's perception of them and their value.

Sucking his teeth, Gotti sat up in his seat. "Fuck is that supposed to mean? You don't trust me to handle myself?"

"No... I don't."

Luciano chuckled but quickly turned it into a choked laugh when Gotti mugged him. He lifted his hands in surrender. "What you mugging me for? He said it."

"Yeah, but you keke-ing like you agree."

"I do. You been real reckless lately and Pops didn't approve. You acting like your other brother was a decade ago, and you saw how that turned out."

With a huff, Gotti crossed his arms over his chest and sat back in his seat. The youngest brother was spoiled and used to getting his way, so his reaction came as no surprise to Gambino.

"Look, you know you earn your keep around here, family or not. You move up based on how loyal you are and by being a big earner. If you can prove I can trust you, I'll put you back in the field and move you up when the time is right."

"What I gotta do?" Gotti asked, expression turning serious.

"I need you to show me that you have discipline, self-control, and focus. If you can control yourself and maintain your priorities, you'll be good. That means stop fucking a different woman every day and stay on your business. I don't care if you go celibate or if you get married. The right woman will influence you, help you focus, and get you further along in life."

Gotti chuckled. "How would you know?"

Luciano released a long breath as he sat up in his seat. If anyone knew how the loss of Kayla effected Gambino, it was his brothers. She was his prize. She made him feel like a winner. He'd been losing ever since. Regardless of his power, money, and status—none of that shit mattered without her. Without his rib.

"I should pop you in your fuckin' mouth," Gambino admitted. "Instead of being a smartass, learn from my mistake. I lost the best woman I ever had because I was out here wilding. Kayla is my rib. She's supposed to protect my heart. I'm out here with no fucking protection. No help. No reward and favor from God. All because I wanted random pussy. The fact that you don't understand that is exactly why I'm sitting you down. If I can't trust you to make wise decisions for yourself, you really expect me to trust you with my soldiers and their teams?"

"Aight, aight," Gotti conceded. "I hear you, big brotha. I apologize. Won't bring it up again."

Gambino released a calming, shaky breath. "Make sure. Because the next time you say some slick shit like that, I might forget you my brother."

"That's gon' be the last time you threaten me without doing something about it," Gotti warned with a smile.

"Aight, that's enough." Luciano shoved Gotti's shoulder and handed him the cigarillo he'd put some of their weed in. "What you need from me, brother?"

Gambino's eyes slowly shifted to Luciano. "I need you as my second in command. I know you enjoy being an enforcer, but I need you mobile. When this nigga gets his shit together, you'll be my consigliere and he will be underboss."

Gotti's eyes widened as he grinned. As much as he didn't want to, Gambino smiled. "You mean that?" Gotti asked, voice light and hopeful. "You'll let me be your second in command?"

"Only if you show me you will be an asset and not a liability."

24

"I will, big brotha. I swear."

Gotti extended his arm across the table, and the brothers shook hands. Gambino looked at Luciano, whose perplexed expression didn't mirror Gotti's excitement. Gambino was aware of the fact that Luciano preferred to get his hands dirty and not handle business. He didn't like to talk and engage with people. Though Gambino respected that, he couldn't deny how intelligent, how wise, his middle brother was. He knew there would be times his judgment would be clouded as the don, and he needed someone he could trust in his ear. Someone he knew would make decisions and offer suggestions that were best for the entire family, not just the brothers.

"I was wondering how this would work with you and Cory. He was Pops' consigliere, but I didn't think he'd be willing to work with you."

Gambino sighed as he accepted the blunt from Gotti. "We talked after the funeral. He is willing to stay on until I find his replacement. He's loyal to the family and the oath he took, so I trust him. I also won't punish him by forcing him to deal with me knowing he doesn't want to. So once the both of you are ready for the new positions, he'll join the board as an advisor and retire from the field."

"That's fair," Luciano said before looking over at Gotti. "I guess it's on you, baby boy. Get your shit together so we can take the cartel to new heights. We owe this to Pops."

Gotti's tongue circled his cheek before he lifted his glass of whisky. "To Pops."

Gambino and Luciano lifted their glasses for a toast. In unison, they all released a low, "To Pops."

Once they finished their drinks and two blunts, the brothers headed downstairs. At the sight of Gambino, Bernie met them by the sitting room.

"How you holding up?" Bernie checked, shaking Luciano's hand.

"I'm maintaining."

"If that's all you can do, do that."

Luciano patted his shoulder and thanked him before walking away and leaving him and Gambino alone.

"I won't hold you. I'm sure you're tired of talking by now." That was so true, all Gambino did was nod with a small smile. "I wanted your approval on something."

"You don't want to wait until I'm officially sworn in?"

Bernie's head shook. "As far as I'm concerned, you're the boss. That's what Samson wanted, so that's what will be."

His words filled Gambino with pride. "I appreciate that. Continue."

"You know I've been working for years to expand my business." That was true. The Nahtahn Cartel had ten smaller cartels that they supplied, and Bernie Lattimore's organization was at the top of that list. Bernie had potential, but his reach was the only thing that kept him from growing. That was part of why Samson wanted to merge the two families. He knew Bernie would benefit from being connected with one of, if not the most powerful, cartels in the underworld of Rose Valley Hills, and the Nahtahns would benefit from Bernie's ties with the secret society.

The secret society was like the checks and balances system of the South. Political plotting, policing and protection, the removal and giving of power. They unofficially ran the government in Rose Valley Hills. They were like a mafia themselves, without the violence. Often, they used the Nahtahn Cartel or the Lowe Mafia if a situation needed someone to get their hands dirty.

So while Bernie had power legally, Samson had it illegally, making them and their children a perfect match.

"Yeah," Gambino agreed. "How can I help?"

"I would like for you to approve an arranged marriage between my family and the Yancy Cartel. It's clear things between you and Kayla are over, and I need an ally."

It was as if Gambino's brain short circuited at the thought of Kayla marrying someone else. They might not have been together for the last eight years, but he found a sense of comfort in the fact that she wasn't married and hadn't had children. Now, her father expected him to approve of her marrying someone else?

As his heart made its way out of the pit of Gambino's stomach, his nostrils flared. "No."

"No?" Bernie repeated. "Why not?"

Why not?

"Kayla is *my* kitten. She's *always* belonged to me. The fuck would make you think I'd *ever* give you permission to give her to someone else?"

5

K ayla

OUT OF RESPECT, KAYLA WENT TO THE DINNER AT
Samson and Claire's home with her father. For her own
peace of mind, she spent most of her time in the library. Her
mind took her back to her visits when Samson would select
a book for her to check out as if it was a real library. When
she came back to return it, he'd make her give him a
summary on what she'd read and learned. Samson understood the value of knowledge, of learning, and he'd instilled
that in his sons as well.

Blinking back tears from the happy memory, her grip
around the glass of cream sherry tightened. At the sound of
loafers on tile, Kayla heightened her view. Her father
leaned against the doorframe with a wide smile.

Why was he so happy?

"I knew I'd find you here. Come downstairs, honey."

Kayla eyed him skeptically before heading in his direction. "What's this about, Papa?"

"I gained approval for your husband."

Her eyes rolled. Though Kayla knew this moment was coming, she wasn't expecting it to come so fast. Even with Kayla accepting her duty to her family, she wasn't happy with the idea of marrying someone she hadn't been in a relationship with. She was blessed by the fact that Bernie allowed her to weigh in on the decision he would make regarding her husband, but now she was confused. The last time they talked about this, they had three options for her to choose from. That was before Samson died and Gambino took over.

Gambino.

He'd actually approved the arranged marriage for her?

Why'd that hurt?

Sure, they were over and had no hope of a future but still... She wasn't expecting the man she used to be in love with to make it easy for her to marry someone else. Then again, Gambino's wild behavior and priority of the cartel was the reason their relationship didn't work. She never came first because of the family. The business. If there was a way he could benefit from the arranged marriage too, it shouldn't have surprised her that he had agreed so quickly.

As they neared the end of the winding stairway, Gambino made his way over to them. He looked devilishly handsome in his bronze colored tuxedo. His wide, tall frame... caramel brown skin with a golden undertone... Gambino could wear a suit like no other—even with the tattoos peeking out of his shirt.

"What's he coming over here for?" she whispered, but Bernie ignored her as he grinned and wrapped his arm around her waist. "Papa..."

"Honey, why didn't you tell me you and Bino rekindled your relationship?"

Gambino shoved his hands into his pockets as a sly smile lifted the corner of his mouth.

"W-what?" she stuttered, turning to look at him.

"He told me you've been talking since the funeral. Had I known that, I wouldn't have asked for approval for you to marry someone else. You can marry Gambino after all."

Kayla's brows wrinkled as she looked at Gambino. His smile widened, drawing her attention to his short beard and medium shaped, pomegranate hued lips. Her body began to shake as anger consumed her confusion.

How dare he suggest they reconnected to keep her from marrying someone else?

The last thing she'd do was disrespect the home or make her father look bad, so as much as she wanted to yell, she stormed away.

Back Home

KAYLA SAT IN THE EGG CHAIR ON THE PATIO OF HER bedroom. Her mother was suffering from the flu, and as much as she wanted to talk to her face to face, she'd been keeping her distance. When she couldn't take it anymore, she left the chilly air and headed inside. Since she left the dinner, she'd been struggling with what her father said and what she wanted to do. A part of her was sure she'd heard him incorrectly, because there was no way Gambino would have lied and suggested they were talking again. What would he get out of that? Her? That couldn't have been the case. He'd made it clear he didn't want her anymore.

30

"Mommy?" she called softly as she stepped into her room. "Are you awake?"

Delilah cleared her throat and weakly tried to sit up in bed. "Yes, but don't come any closer. Do you have on a mask?"

"No, but I'll be fine. I wanted to talk to you about what happened at the dinner tonight."

After a brief coughing spell, Delilah asked, "What did I miss?"

"Well... the strangest thing happened. You know Papa and I have been going over the choices for my husband, right? Because I couldn't be born into a normal family with a normal family business and be a doctor or lawyer. No, I have to be a don's wife—"

"Kayla," Delilah whined before coughing.

"Okay, alright. So at the dinner, he told me he had approval for my husband."

"Who did he choose?"

"That's what has me confused. He suggested I was going to marry Gambino." She paused as her mouth twisted to the side. "Well, he said that I could marry him after all."

"Hmm... Why would he say that?"

"That's why it was so strange because nothing has happened between us. Well, he did apologize at the funeral. For some reason, Papa seems to think we've been talking since then."

"Is that what Gambino t-told—" Delilah sneezed and groaned.

"I don't know why he would say that because it isn't true. Maybe Papa misunderstood him. I left abruptly because I was confused and upset, so I didn't have time to ask any questions."

"Well, when he gets home, ask him exactly what the

both of them said. Let me know when I wake back up, and we can take it from there."

"Okay, Mommy. Do you need anything?"

"Just sleep. I feel horrible."

With a smile, Kayla nodded her agreement. "Yes, ma'am. I'll let you rest."

"I love you."

"I love you too."

Kayla made her way back to her room with her thoughts in a blur. Maybe she misheard. Maybe Bernie misunderstood. Regardless, something was wrong, and tomorrow, she'd figure out what.

6

G ambino

IT WAS THE LAST EVENING OF SAMSON'S CELEBRATION of life, and it was the most relaxed event of the week. They'd rented out a ballroom for a casino night, and so far, everyone had been having a good time. When Gambino approached Gotti and Kayla, it wasn't his intention to eavesdrop. However, hearing the tail end of their conversation piqued his interest and held him back.

"Tell me what *you* think, sis," Gotti requested. "You're the only woman outside of Mommy that I trust."

A smirk lifted the left side of Gambino's mouth. He loved the close bond his family had with Kayla back in the day. It made the breakup awkward because they kept in touch with her even after she cut him off. Kayla gave him an innocent kiss on the cheek then wrapped her arm around him, and Gotti melted against her. His head rested on her shoulder.

"I think he's right. Do you know who you are? The power and potential you have? If you locked in, you'd be unstoppable, Gotti."

"But a wife? Fuck is I'm supposed to do with that?"

Kayla giggled as she rested her head against his. "First, *that* should be *her*. You're talking about a human being not an object, so you won't be able to treat her like one. Second, protect her and spoil her and let her influence you and be a source of peace for you. I don't think there's a rush on that, right? Maybe you should just focus on taking better care of yourself now and wait until he arranges a marriage for you, because apparently, that's what he does now."

Clearing his throat, Gambino walked in front of them and made his presence known. Something in her eyes flickered as she stared at him. Her expression hardened but she didn't say anything, and her self control amused Gambino.

"You haven't cursed me out or tried to hit me yet," Gambino acknowledged.

That made her soften. "I've learned to keep my hands to myself, thank you."

"In all occasions? Because I know a few that would warrant having your hands all over me."

Her eyes rolled and she scoffed as Gotti chuckled and excused himself from the conversation.

"I would never disrespect you in public. Not now that you're..." Her hand motioned toward him as she struggled with the title.

"Now that I'm what?"

"You know who you are."

"Yeah, but I want to hear you say it."

Quite frankly, she didn't have to say the title. Gambino

would've been good just hearing her say his name. She used to say it with a honeyed sweetness that always made him smile... even when she said it while they were arguing.

"You're the don," she acknowledged. "The boss of all bosses." Kayla stood. "And the man who approved an arranged marriage for me, but I'm confused on who my husband will be. It can't be you. What did you and Papa discuss last night?"

Gambino looked around, and when his eyes settled on the changing rooms for brides and grooms who used the ballroom, he told her, "Let's go somewhere private so we can talk."

Kayla followed behind him, keeping space between them just as she did at the funeral. When they were in the room alone, his eyes scanned every inch of her. She was even more beautiful now than she was in the past. The weight she'd gained settled in all the right places, and the five-eight beauty had on six inch heels, making her just a few inches shorter than him. At six-six, Gambino loved Kayla's height. It was one of the first things, outside of her face, that attracted him. Her having the perfect amount of hips and ass was an extra bonus.

She was dressed in an all-silk ensemble that clung to her curves perfectly. Her wavy hair flowed loosely, light makeup covered her face, and she smelled good—warm, like lavender and citrus.

Gambino couldn't stop himself from closing the space between them. He heard the sharp intake of breath she took as his nose slid up her neck and into her hair.

"You smell... so good." Her hands trembled as she grabbed his arms and gently pushed him away. Confusion filled him and covered his face as he asked, "Are you afraid of me now?"

"No. I just would prefer it if you stayed out of my personal space."

With a smile, Gambino nodded and took a step back to grant her request.

"Go ahead then. Let me have it."

Her mouth opened and closed before she spoke. "What did you and Papa discuss last night?"

"He asked me to approve a marriage between you and the Yancy Cartel."

"Oh." Her eyes blinked rapidly and brows wrinkled as if she was confused by his words. Releasing a low chuckle, she rubbed the pads of her fingers together. "I'm surprised. We said we'd pick together. I wonder why he chose them."

"Doesn't matter. I told him no."

"Why?" she asked quietly.

"Because the both of you are out your fuckin' minds if you think I'm going to sign off on you marrying anyone else."

Chuckling, Kayla took a step in his direction. "You don't get to decide that. I don't care if you're the don or not, you have *no* say in my personal life anymore."

"Kitten, I—"

"Don't call me that!" she yelled, eyes watering. "You hurt me! You tossed what we had aside like it meant nothing! I loved you, and you just..."

Her chin trembled as she fought to keep her tears in. Kayla groaned when they fell, as if she was upset she expressed herself in front of him. Cupping her cheek, Gambino wiped away her tears. He tilted her head, and her eyes closed.

"You hurt me," she repeated, and that time, more tears fell.

"I'm sorry, kitten." Wiping her tears away turned into

36

kissing them away. His hands lowered to her waist. "I'm sorry." His hands lowered to her ass. She moaned when he squeezed it. "I promise I won't do it again."

"Your promises mean nothing to me."

Resting her forehead on his, Gambino sighed. "Let me fix this. Fix us. I want you, and I need you, Kayla."

Her head shook adamantly as she pulled away. "No. I don't trust you."

"And I get that," Gambino said cautiously. Softly. It was an active practice maintaining gentleness with her when he was groomed to be hard, but she was worth it. "I know my words don't matter, but I'm a changed man. That version of me you had eight years ago no longer exists. I get that you don't trust *him*." Her backward steps caused her to bump into the wall. "I'm asking you to get to know and trust *me*."

She swallowed her words and tugged her fingers. Her nervous tell. It was a good thing she didn't sit at any of the poker tables that night.

"I did tell an untruth," Gambino combined. "It's not a practice I make a habit out of, but hearing that Bernie wanted you to marry someone else knocked me off my square. I told him that we were talking again just to halt the process. If you want nothing to do with me..."

He couldn't even allow the words to tumble out of his mouth.

He couldn't lie and say he'd let her go, because he wouldn't. Now that he had her back in his life, there was no way he'd let her leave again.

"What? You'll let me go?" she asked sweetly.

"*Hell* no." The words fell quickly, making her snicker. She tugged her bottom lip between her teeth as he took another step toward her. "You will be mine. You *are* mine.

I'll just... give you a wing at the house and keep my distance until you're ready for me to fix things between us."

"So Papa wasn't wrong last night? You told him we could get married?"

"I did." He took the last step to close the distance between them. "Wanna hit me now?"

Her eyes fluttered before focusing on his lips. "No," she whispered. "I don't want to hit you."

His tone lowered when he asked, "Then what do you want to do? Hmm?"

"I..." Kayla's eyes shifted to his before lowering to his lips. She licked hers before huffing. "I—"

Resting his hand against the wall, Gambino lowered his lips to hers. He pulled away to gauge her response. Her hand wrapped around his neck, and she used it to pull him back to her. The kiss was slow, deep, and tender. So slow, so deep, and so tender, his dick hardened and heart softened. Her body weakened against him, and Gambino wrapped his arm around her to hold her up. Each sigh and whimper she released against his mouth made his heart and dick throb. All it took was one brush of her hips against his.

Gambino pulled his shaft out of his boxers and jeans before pushing her panties to the side underneath her dress and picking her up. The only reason he pulled away from the kiss was because he wanted to look into her eyes as he filled her. She moaned and bit down on her bottom lip as her nails dug into his shoulders.

Gambino wondered if his return to her pussy was how it felt to eat after a forty day fast. How it felt to drink water after being in a desert. How it felt to return home after a long voyage. In his case, the voyage had been eight years. If Gambino had it his way, he'd never be away from her that long again.

As he stroked her against the wall, Gambino returned his lips to hers. She was so fucking wet, he was sure his jeans would be soaked with her juices and cum.

"Oh God," she moaned as her back arched and legs tightened around him.

"Don't praise Him. *I'm* the one making this pussy leak. Call *my* fuckin' name."

"Gambino," she sang through trembling lips. "You feel so good."

Groaning, Gambino picked up the pace as he buried his face in her neck. Her hums. Her moans. Her whimpers. He collected each sound she made in his heart. Kayla's walls tightened around him. She gasped before releasing a hiss. Gambino switched from one nipple to the other, making her pussy wetter.

"Oh my Go—Gambino."

"Hmm? I missed you and this wet ass pussy." He kissed her face. "I missed hearing you say my name." He kissed her lips. "I missed making you cum."

"Bino, please, I-I can't take anymore."

"You can and you will. I'ma take good care of you. Just breathe. Daddy got you."

"Hmm... ah!" Her eyes squeezed shut as she whined, "Bino, baby..."

Her walls throbbed against him as she came.

"Mm, fuck." Gambino had to keep himself from cumming with her. He grunted and tightened his hold on her as she bucked against him and cried out his name. When he couldn't hold back anymore, he filled her with his seeds and prayed a baby would sprout and bloom.

Once they both were composed, he pulled out and set her on her feet.

"I know this is a lot," Gambino said, "but if you're willing to let me earn your trust, do as I say tonight, okay?"

Her mouth twisted to the side as she thought over his words. Eventually, she nodded her agreement. "Okay."

Gambino placed a kiss on her forehead and told her to wait there. When he made it back to the ballroom, he booked Kayla a suite at *The Rose Valley Hotel*, then told Bernie that his daughter would not be returning home.

7

K ayla

KAYLA PACED THE CARPETED FLOOR OF THE SUITE. When she agreed to follow Gambino's lead last night, she didn't expect it to end with her spending the night at a hotel alone. That was probably for the best, because she couldn't believe she'd had sex with him so easily. For years, her hurt and anger burned like an open flame. How could she allow him to get close enough to touch her so easily?

At the sound of knocking, Kayla walked over to the door. She'd used the products in her suite to freshen up, but she was filled with relief to see her father holding her luggage and toiletry bag.

"Whew, I'm glad I keep a bag packed for every season," she said, accepting the toiletry bag and a hug from her father as he released a robust laugh.

"I bet. I don't think you would have wanted me to pack

this for you while your mom is sick."

"Not at all. No offense, Papa, but if Mommy didn't pick out your clothes, you'd be walking around like a middle aged Steve Urkel."

His laughter increased as the door closed behind him. "Not too much on your old man now."

"Oh Jesus. Who taught you that?"

"I'm hip. I be on the Tok."

"The Tok?" she released before sputtering a choked laugh as they walked into the small kitchen area of the suite. "Yeah, okay, Papa."

After fixing him a plate of the French toast, bacon, and fruit she'd ordered from room service, they sat down. For a few seconds, he just stared at her in awe.

"I'm happy you and Bino are back together. I always knew our families could be great together."

"Whoa, Papa. We're not together." Her head hung and voice grew quiet as she confessed, "I don't know what we are, but we're not together."

"Do you... not want to marry him?"

"Do I really have a choice?"

"Of course you have a choice."

"Do I? Because he told me you wanted to marry me off to the Yancy Cartel. I thought we agreed to decide together?"

"We did but... Carmichael approached me after the funeral and the deal he wanted to make... I couldn't pass it up. No one beyond the Nahtahns were able to offer a partnership as good as the one the Yancys could provide. So if you're saying you don't want to be with Gambino—"

"Papa, he's not going to let me marry Carmichael." Sighing, Kayla massaged her temple. "I understand how important who I marry is to the family and business. I know in my mind the Nahtahns are the best choice but my heart... I don't know. Maybe my expectations were too high. Maybe I messed my own self up actually falling in love with him. Things between us should have been just a business arrangement. If they were, we'd be married and—"

"And you'd probably be miserable. For what it's worth, Gambino has changed with time. He's a man of integrity now. However you decide to navigate the waters of your marriage that's up to you, but business or not, if you ever want to get out... just let me know."

Appreciating the sentiment, Kayla nodded, and they turned their attention to the food. She honestly had no idea what she was going to do, but from the looks of it, the decision for her to marry Gambino was already made... even if her father hadn't realized it.

Three Days Later

KAYLA LOOKED OVER THE DINNERWARE ON THE DINING room table. She was picked up from the hotel in a town car and taken back to the Nahtahn estate. The ten bedroom mansion set in the center of twenty acres of land. It was the biggest home in the Nahtahn Cove. The one Samson and Claire shared. Now that he was gone, it belonged to the new don and his future family. Kayla called Claire as soon as she heard the news from the house manager to insist they stay somewhere else, but Claire assured her that she'd be living with her sister regardless because she didn't want to be in the large home alone.

It had been completely cleared out—down to the art on the walls. Kayla had spent the day working with several designers to fill the mansion with new art and furniture for her and Gambino and getting to know the house staff, which included a manager, groundsman, butler and maid, and three alternating chefs. She already knew the guards from her visits over the years and felt more comfortable than she thought she would.

Gambino sauntered into the room, looking as sexy as ever in a crisp burgundy suit. As he loosened his tie, Kayla couldn't help but notice the tired look on his face. Still, she couldn't deny her frustration over how things had been going between them. It went against her nature to bite her tongue, even with Gambino. It may have made her ill prepared for his lifestyle and to be his wife, but she didn't care. She wouldn't change her character for *anyone*. A part of her wanted to believe he didn't mean that when he said it eight years ago, but it stung and implanted itself in her mind and heart every day over the years.

"We need to talk," she informed him. "I feel like I have no control of my life. You're not letting me in on anything. One minute I'm in a hotel and the nex—"

Gambino grabbed her hair and used it to tilt her head for a kiss that made her nipples harden and pussy leak. He moaned against her mouth as he wrapped his arms around her. She'd never understood the term kissed senseless until he pulled away and there was not a single thought in her mind.

With a smirk, Gambino caressed her cheek. Clearing her throat, Kayla forced herself to focus.

"Was that your way of shutting me up?" she asked.

"Yes, but I've also wanted to kiss you all day. For the past eight years actually. I need to make up for lost time."

His confession made her smile. "That was sweet."

"That was the truth." His hand went to hers and he put

it against his hardened dick. "The thought of coming home to you has had me like this all day."

The more he talked, the softer she became.

"Bino." With a sigh, Kayla ran her fingers through her hair. "You're making this hard."

"Can't be harder than me." When she blushed, he added, "Whatever it is, we'll talk it through and work it out."

His statement gave her confidence, so she nodded her agreement. "I guess we can talk later. After you've had time to wind down."

"How about over dinner?"

"Sounds good."

They parted ways, and her mind went to her parents when she was growing up. How long and hard her father's days were and how her mother took pride in making their home a place of peace for him when he arrived. She swore Bernie gave her every one of her heart's desires, and making his house feel like a peaceful home in exchange was a small price to pay.

Kayla huffed and went toward the master bedroom. Gambino turned and eyed her inquisitively as he pulled his tie off.

"What's wrong?"

Ignoring his question, she undressed him. When she was done, she ran the water for him to take a shower. After he got out, she had his whisky and blunt filled cigarillo waiting. With a kiss to his cheek, she told him to enjoy himself before attempting to leave, but Gambino used her wrist to pull her onto his lap. He kissed her neck and further relaxed in the reclining chair that was in the sitting area of the bedroom.

"Thank you. All the shit that was on my mind when I

got home instantly melted away because of what you just did."

"I'm glad I could help. It wasn't my intention to come off so combative when you first got here. I was just overwhelmed."

"I can understand that. A lot has been changing lately. We can talk about it now if you'd like."

Her head shook as she lit the blunt for him. "No, it's fine. I can wait."

"I'm relaxed now, kitten. What's on your mind?"

"You didn't—" She pulled in a deep breath and rephrased what she wanted to say in her head so it wouldn't sound like she was complaining. "I don't know what's happening. You haven't actually asked me to marry you. I was dropped off at the hotel then brought here. I wouldn't have known what was going on with my things if Braxton hadn't told me they were going to be delivered from the house soon. I'm just... feeling very unsure right now."

"I hear you, and I apologize if my actions have overwhelmed you. I'm used to making decisions now and having everyone follow my lead, and I inadvertently did that with you. The stay at the hotel was to give me time to have the estate cleared out and the designers here so they could decorate and design it to your liking. It wasn't my intention to shut you out. I just wanted to take care of you and please you."

"I see that now and I appreciate it, but I'd also appreciate it if you'd communicate with me. I know we can't talk about everything, but I'd at least like to know what's going on in our home. I'm more than willing to follow your lead but it's easier when I know where you're taking me."

His lips formed a smile before they said, "I can do that." Then he kissed her. "As far as me not asking you to marry me, I wasn't aware that I had to. I assumed I made it perfectly clear that you were mine at the ballroom."

"Well yes, but... Shouldn't we discuss what kind of marriage we're going to have? I think it'll be safer for me if it was just a business arrangement."

Gambino fell into a fit of laughter until he was at the point of tears. The longer he laughed, the more irritated Kayla got. Eventually, she accepted the fact that he didn't take her seriously—at all.

"I know you can't possibly mean physically, so I assume you're talking about your heart?" She nodded. "I won't keep telling you that you're safe with me. That I've changed and that you can trust me. I'll just show you. This will be a real marriage though. Love, romance, sex, babies... I'm with all that." His rough tone softened when he added, "And though you may be scared to admit it, I know you are too."

"Honestly... I've been too scared to allow myself to believe this was real. That it was happening. The way things ended between us was brutal and I'm not trying to punish you for something I should have already forgiven you for, but I also can't act like this isn't hard." She cupped his cheek as her eyes watered. "I wanted nothing more than to spend my life with you and that day was traumatizing. Not just because of the way you spoke to me but finding out that you'd cheated too. I can admit that I do want this to work, but I'm scared you'll hurt me again. You already cheated once and I can't, I won't deal with that again."

He was gentler than she expected. She expected this to turn into an argument because she was speaking her mind. Instead, Gambino held her waist and stared into her eyes lovingly for seconds on end before he responded.

"I know, kitten, and I wouldn't put you in the position to have to. I value you and fidelity now. I don't want to lose you, true, but I don't want to go to war with God because I hurt you. I do enough shit for Him to have to forgive. I don't want hurting you to be moved up to the top of the list." She smiled. "I have discipline now, and I'm not moved by pussy or my flesh. All I ask is that you be patient with me, and I'll show you and take care of the rest."

It was easier to believe Gambino hadn't changed. The more she got inside his mind and heart, the more Kayla realized he wasn't the same.

"What do you say?" he asked.

Her response? Dropping to her knees and pulling his dick out of his boxers. Her hand ran up the length of his long, curved shaft before she took him into her mouth. The wetter it got, the more vocal he became.

"That's good, kitten. Hide my dick in your mouth."

She moaned against him, and Gambino grunted as his stomach clenched. He pulled in a sizzling breath and fisted her hair as she took him as far down her throat as he could go. Wrist work allowed her to stroke him each time he came out of her mouth. She plopped the head out and ran her tongue across it before swallowing him.

"Fuck!" he roared, tightening his grip on her hair. "You tryna swallow my babies huh? I'ma give you about three or four of 'em if you keep fuckin' around."

Kayla giggled. "Be quiet and don't distract me until after I make you cum."

"Yes, Kayla. Whatever you say."

She laughed again but quickly regrouped and tightened her suction on his shaft. Not long passed before he did just what he said and shot his cum down her throat. As soon as she pulled her head up, Gambino picked her up and carried her to the bed.

"I need you," he muttered, all but ripping her wrap

dress from her body.

Kayla was still getting used to him being so expressive and communicative. Both turned her on. She spread her legs wide as he made his way between them. Their eyes locked as he swiped his thick tongue between her folds. Her body melted against the bed as she tightened her grip on her legs.

"Mm, she so wet and pretty." Gambino lightly spanked her pussy, and she cried out. The friction against her clit made her pussy throb. "Oh, you like that?"

"Yes, daddy." She bit down on her bottom lip. "Do it again."

"Say please."

"*Please*, baby. Please do it again."

He did it again, and again, and again... until he unlocked a new kink and made her cum. Her legs were still shaking when he finally slurped her clit into his mouth. "Ah, Biiino," she whined, feeling her walls contract again. "That's it. Eat me. Lick all that cum up."

He growled against her opening before swirling his tongue around it. "Yesss, Gambino. Clean up the mess you made." He smacked the side of her ass before choking her. She panted as he tightened his grip around her neck and slithered his tongue from left to right.

"Why you quiet now?" he taunted before sucking her clit. "Keep talking that shit," Gambino commanded before licking her clit again.

But she couldn't. Not while she came. It wasn't until the aftershocks passed through her that she was able to think and breathe let alone speak. His chuckle was cocky as he slid up her frame. Kayla wasted no time wrapping her arms around him and connecting her lips with his. She moaned against his lips as he stretched and filled her.

Gambino broke the kiss to look at the connection of them. As he filled her with deep, hard strokes, he muttered, "Look at what I'm doing to this pussy." She whimpered. "Look at how wet she is. Does she want to cum for me?"

Kayla nodded as her lips trembled. Her back arched as she prepared for the overwhelming sensation that was about to consume her. Their eyes remained locked until hers rolled into the back of her head as she came.

"You still love me, kitten?" he asked, tilting her body and hitting her spot with each stroke. "You said you loved me at the ballroom. *Loved.*" As he increased his pace, Gambino placed emphasis on the D.

"Ohmygod," she slurred, pushing into his stomach as the sound of her wetness filled the room. She'd be squirting in a matter of seconds.

"Do you love me?"

"Yes!" she cried out as she squirted, body convulsing as his hand alternated between rubbing her clit and opening each time he pulled out. Whines and whimpers escaped her. Each time he pulled out and drilled back into her she gasped for air.

"Tell me you love me."

"I love you, Gambino," Kayla almost cried, squeezing her eyes shut. When she covered her face with her palms, he slowed his strokes. Lowering himself to her, he went just as deep.

"Kitten." He gently pulled her hands down, but she avoided his eyes. "Your love won't be taken advantage of or wasted." Her eyes connected with his. "And I love you... so much more."

Cupping his bearded cheeks, she lowered him to her lips as her tears fell. She wrapped her legs around him and never wanted to let him go.

8

G ambino

"I want to sit on your face."

The randomness of Kayla's statement caught him off guard. They'd had dinner and were resting in their Alaskan king bed. For whatever reason, she thought she'd be sleeping in a different room. Gambino understood that he told her he'd give her her own wing of the estate if it was necessary, but that was before she sucked his soul out of his dick and told him that she still loved him.

"Climb up, kitten." He tossed his phone onto the bed. "Come put that pretty pussy on my face."

She straddled him, and Gambino moaned into her pussy as he gripped her ass cheeks and squeezed. As he buried himself in her wetness, Gambino decided he was content with that being his final place of rest. Kayla rocked against him, riding his face in a slow pace that allowed him to lick every inch of her. Her body trembled, and she released quiet moans and chants of his name.

Kayla hissed as he smacked her ass then slid his hands up her back. "I'm about to cum, Bino."

Gambino massaged her breasts and twisted her nipples. His tongue brushed against her opening and her clit until she saturated his mouth and chin with her cum. As she climbed down him, his phone vibrated.

"Are you going to answer that?" she asked, wiping his face.

"I should, but I don't want to."

Her smile was warm as she handed him his phone. As he answered, Kayla slid down on his dick, reminding him of why he used to love sleeping naked with her.

"Hel—*shit*."

"You good?" Gotti asked.

For a few seconds, the sight of her riding him was a complete distraction. When she gripped her breasts and squeezed before lifting one and licking her nipple, Gambino shuddered and moaned.

"Bino!" Gotti yelled into the receiver.

"Y-yeah, wassup?" Gambino replied, grabbing her waist as she bounced up and down on his dick with a medium pace. There was no doubt in his mind that his brother had to hear the sound of her fat ass smacking against him each time she came down. "You good, baby boy?"

"Yeah, but the warehouse on Robbin Ave. ain't. It was bombed."

"What!" Gambino pushed Kayla off him gently and climbed out of the bed.

"Just get down here, big brotha. *Now*."

The growl Gambino released as he charged toward the closet came from deep within his throat. By the time he was done grabbing sweatpants and a hoodie, Kayla was walking toward him with a warm, soapy towel. When she cleaned his dick, she stroked it instead of simply wiping it. The sensual act made his body loosen.

"Relax," she commanded softly. "Whatever it is, you can handle it. But you won't be able to fix it if you aren't thinking straight. Stay calm, baby."

Cupping her cheek, Gambino tilted her head and kissed her passionately. "Thank you. I needed this, because I was about to go on a fuckin' rampage."

"I can tell," she acknowledged through her giggle as she released him. "You're scariest when you're silent."

He watched as she grabbed a pair of boxers for him out of the drawer. All he could do was shake his head as he dressed quickly. Could he have done life as the don without her? Yes. Did he want to? Absolutely not.

At the Warehouse

GAMBINO WALKED THE LENGTH OF THE WAREHOUSE with his brothers. Twenty thousand square feet... burned to the ground. By day, the warehouse was used for exporting and importing legal goods. Companies were able to rent space in the warehouse and used the eighteen wheelers to send their products anywhere in the world. By night, the warehouse was used to break down and pack up drugs. When the bomb went off, it was full of Nahtahn Cartel workers. Of the seventy eight men and women that were inside, only four survived.

When Luciano covered his mouth and nose and coughed, Gambino decided that was enough. They went out to their separate cars and drove to the twenty-four hour diner on the corner of the street. There, Cory met them. Gambino decided to address him first, because he knew Cory wouldn't want to be around him for long.

"Do we have any idea who did this?"

Cory's head shook. "No, but the attack isn't a surprise. Any time a new don is sworn in there's a chance enemies arise."

"Or partners who want to try and take over," Luciano added, and Cory nodded his agreement.

"The camera footage," Gambino started, but Gotti nodded and cut him off.

"We don't have anything now, but I assume the bomb was planted before today. I can try and see if the team will be able to access previous footage."

As much as Gambino wanted to tell his brother to stand down, maybe this would be a good test for Gotti to see if would focus and come through.

"Alright, do that. I want the funerals of those we lost tonight taken care of. The families too."

"On it," Luciano said, pulling out his burner phone.

"I would advise doing sweeps of every building in your possession," Cory said, flagging the waitress down to order a cup of coffee. "It's likely this was a onetime message, but to be safe, you need to get ahead of this. The legal and illegal businesses."

Gambino nodded his agreement. "I assume the police have already been on the scene?"

"Yeah," Gotti confirmed. "I waited until they left to call you. Lu was the second to arrive."

His response caught Gambino by surprise, and he was unable to hold his smile back. As the don, only whispered assumptions about Gambino's role in the Nahtahn Cartel were allowed. He was supposed to always keep his hands clean, and when possible, remain a ghost. Should the entire organization be brought up on RICO charges that night, a sign of a well-run business was Gambino's name not being attached to *anything*.

The men talked a little while longer and had a late breakfast before making plans to rebuild. As they headed out, Gambino gripped Gotti by the back of his neck and pulled him close.

"I'm proud of you, baby boy. Keep making decisions like you did tonight and I might put you back in action. I know your teams are missing you, and you've proven they trust your lead when it comes down to the warehouses. I've taken notice."

"Aye, I 'preciate that, big brotha. For real."

Gambino dropped a kiss to Gotti's temple before they embraced, then he and Luciano did the same. As he headed home, his mind raced. It was easy deciding what needed to be done, but the work wasn't finished yet. The next several months would be crazy while they tried to rebuild. Gambino now had two focuses: finding out who planted the bomb and making sure they didn't strike again.

9

K ayla
One Week Later

KAYLA COULDN'T IGNORE THE DISAPPOINTED expression that covered Claire's face. She'd stopped by the estate to visit her sons and none of them were there. Braxton, the house manager, had reminded both Kayla and Gambino and had it on their personal calendars, but her son was in the wind.

Claire's eyes watered at the sight of the flowers and card Kayla had waiting for her. It wasn't an expensive present, but she wanted Claire to know she'd been thinking of her since her husband's passing.

"These are beautiful, Kayla. Thank you." After kissing Kayla's cheek, Claire looked around the kitchen for Brandy, Braxton's sister and one of the private chefs. "Brandy, do you mind grabbing me a vase from the pantry if that's where they still are?"

"They are," Kayla confirmed. "We switched out the furniture, but the library, closet spaces, and pantries are still the same."

Claire sighed as she nodded and picked up her glass of wine. The women walked into the sunroom, and Kayla avoided cutting the TV on immediately since it looked like Claire had something on her mind.

"You wanna talk about it?" Kayla asked softly as she pulled her legs under her in the large chair.

"My sons forgot about me." Claire chuckled and shook her head. "I know that sounds dramatic, but I was looking forward to seeing all three of them today."

"I'm sorry. They've been running around like crazy but that's no excuse."

"You're not the one that should be apologizing, sweetheart."

"Do you want me to call Bino and see where they are?"

Claire shook her head as she took a sip of her wine. "No, I'm sure it's important if all three of them missed my visit. I'll be fine."

"Well, I know I can't take their place, but I'll be here all day if you want to hang out. We can go shopping. Gambino added me to all of his cards."

They both grinned sneakily before bursting into a fit of laughter. "How are you adjusting to being here? Being with my baby? Did you two actually reconnect after the funeral?"

Kayla's eyes rolled as her head shook. "We did not. He lied."

"I figured so. I figured if the two of you were going to reconcile that you'd tell me."

"I definitely would have. It was a surprise to me. But...

I'm adjusting well. How about you? Did you really want to give this beautiful home up?"

Claire's smile was bitter before she downed the rest of her wine. "It wasn't a home without my husband and sons. My sister's home is giving me peace. I don't regret my decision at all." Her hand stretched across the space between their chairs and covered Kayla's. "Besides, the official Nahtahn Estate is for the don and his wife, and that will soon be you and Gambino. That role, those shoes, that is a big responsibility for you to fill. I'll be here whenever you need me."

"I know, and I appreciate that. I don't think I've fully wrapped my head around what it all means yet. Up until a couple of weeks ago, I'd long ago rejected the idea that I'd ever be in this position with Gambino. I still can't believe we're together again."

"I'm glad you gave him another chance, and I want you to know I don't condone cheating. What he did had nothing to do with you and everything to do with him. His insecurities. What he lacked as a man. He's found that now, and there's no doubt in my mind that he will take care of you. But if he ever starts to show his ass, don't you hesitate to call me."

"Yes, ma'am," Kayla agreed through her chuckle.

They continued to talk for another hour or so before deciding to go shopping and have dinner, and the only thing that would have made it better for Kayla was if her mother would have been able to join them too.

Three Days Later

LIGHT TAPS AGAINST THE LIBRARY DOOR GAINED Kayla's attention. She truly loved to read and spent most of her time in that room. It also made her feel closer to Samson. Though she'd never had to work a day in her life, if she had to, she'd be a librarian. Her dream was to own her own bookstore one day.

"Come in," she granted, closing the book she was reading and pulling her legs from under her.

Kayla smiled at the sight of Brandy. "I wanted to let you know that dinner is almost ready. First course is already on the table. Mr. Nahtahn will be joining you this evening."

"Oh." Kayla's head jolted at the announcement. She hadn't seen Gambino in what felt like forever. He left early and came in late, prompting him to sleep in one of the guest bedrooms every night. "Thanks for letting me know."

"My pleasure."

Instead of heading straight down to the dining room, Kayla slipped out of her robe and gown, putting on a form fitting Joah Brown maxi slit dress. She sprayed a few spritzes of YSL Libre Intense against her body, slipped into a pair of matching heeled sandals, then went downstairs.

A low gasp escaped her at the sight of Gambino. She didn't know he was already there. Her eyes misted at the sight of him. How she'd gone from not wanting to look at him to feeling overwhelmed with joy at the sight of him was a question she didn't have the answer for.

He stood after setting his glass of brown liquor down and eyed her frame slowly. "My God." His Adam's apple bobbed as she sashayed toward the table. The mesh dress wasn't see through, but it was thin enough for him to be able to tell she didn't have on underwear. "I'm fucking you tonight. Bring your sexy ass here."

Kayla's laugh was soft as she made her way into his

arms. He lowered himself to her neck and nuzzled her, tickling her with his beard. As his hands lowered to her ass, he looked into her eyes and said, "I've missed you," before giving her a sloppy, nasty kiss that his tongue led.

"Mm," she moaned against him, running her hands down his back, then pulling him close. "I've missed you too, baby. After dinner, I'm going to show you just how much."

His smile was soft as he pushed her hair off her shoulders and cupped her face. "I need to apologize."

"For what?"

Instead of answering her quickly, Gambino motioned for her to sit in the chair that was next to his. The common rooms had been Kayla's favorite to decorate. She stuck to gold, cream, and crystal... giving the large dining room an opulent vibe. Gambino poured her a glass of wine and refilled his whisky before he continued.

"You knew what you were doing putting this dress on," he muttered, eyes lowering to her D-cups. "I can't keep my eyes off you, kitten. I'm tempted to push this food off the table and have *you* for dinner."

Her hand gently cupped his chin, and she used it to guide his eyes to hers. "What do you feel you need to apologize for?"

"The lack of my presence." Kayla smiled as her body neared his. She didn't realize how anxious his statement made her until he clarified. *"When you love someone, the best thing you can offer is your presence. How can you love if you are not there?"*

Her eyes closed and she inhaled a deep breath as he quoted one of her favorite quotes from Thich Nhat Hanh.

"You remembered," she muttered as he caressed her cheek with his thumb. Her face shifted slightly, and she kissed his palm.

"I remember everything about you, Kayla."

Finding his eyes, she confessed, "It's okay. Don't get me wrong, I appreciate you coming home for dinner, but I know how this lifestyle works. I know the role you play, and that the cartel comes first. I will get used to missing your presence."

Gambino's head shook as he took her hands into his. "The cartel doesn't come first. You do. However, realistically, when things like what happened a week ago happen, it will take more of my time. But I wanted to apologize for the lack of my presence and be here with you tonight. This isn't the start of our reconnection that I wanted. I haven't even been able to take you on a date yet."

"I appreciate your mindfulness, but I don't want you to feel bad about it. I want to spend quality time with you, but I know you're busy right now."

"I appreciate that. I'll do better. Dinner tonight, and I will take you out tomorrow after my meeting. Once we figure out who's behind the bomb, we can take a trip."

"Bomb!" she shrieked quietly, snatching her hands out of his. "What the hell, Bino? There was a bomb? That's why you rushed out of here that night? Was anyone hurt?"

"Relax, kitten," he ordered softly with a smile as he took her hands into his. "I don't want to discuss that with you. I don't want you worried. We're handling it though."

Kayla released a shaky breath as she nodded. "Alright. I won't worry. Just promise me that you'll be careful and make sure my brothers are too. If anything happened to you —I just got you back."

"Hey," he spoke softly, pulling her lips to his when her tears threatened to pour. After kissing her three times, he set her on his lap. "You know who you belong to. I won't lie and say what I'm doing is safe." Gambino caught a tear before it could fall. "What I will say is, I'm doing everything in my power to annihilate threats and enemies before they can bring us any harm. I promise to do everything I can to *always* come home to you."

With a nod, Kayla wrapped her arms around his neck and rested her face against his. They sat like that for a while in silence, enjoying the other's closeness. Eventually, they began to eat when the second course was brought out, but Gambino kept her on his lap the whole time.

10

Gambino

THE MOMENT FELT SURREAL AS GAMBINO SAT BEHIND his father's desk, in his study, and conducted business. He kept forcing himself to stay present and not lose his focus because of his grief. Samson Nahtahn was one of the deadliest men Gambino knew. For a heart attack to have taken him out... Gambino wasn't sure if that was grace or a fucking joke.

"None of these men are big enough threats to pull off a bomb," Gambino said, tossing the pictures onto the desk. "How are your guys coming along with the camera footage?"

"They haven't seen anything suspicious yet," Gotti answered. "So far, they've gone through about a week's worth of footage and they haven't seen anyone plant anything."

"An outsider wouldn't have been able to get past guards," Gambino remembered.

"That's true," Luciano agreed. "So it either had to be someone dropping something off or someone they were expecting."

"It was an inside job," Gambino said. "I feel it in my gut. One of the workers crossed us for someone else. I need a list of everyone who was working for the past month. Highlight whoever was there that day and left early. For the sake of fairness, look into any deliveries we had as well. Postal, food, whatever."

"On it," Luciano agreed. "But there is one other thing."

"Wassup?"

Luciano looked over at Gotti as he released a hard breath. "I don't know a lot about it, but Cory mentioned Pops had looked into arranged marriages."

"For who?" Gambino asked, chin jutted.

"Us. You were first."

Not bothering to respond, Gambino pulled out the burner phone that had a secure line and dialed Cory's number.

"Yeah?" Cory answered with music and wind blowing in the background. Gambino waited until he lowered it to speak.

"Pops was looking into arranged marriages for us?"

"Yeah... but he ended up changing his mind. For Gotti at least."

Gambino smiled as he put the call on speakerphone. "You said he wanted to do arranged marriages but changed his mind about Gotti?"

Gotti's head jerked and eyes widened as if the words physically struct him.

"Yeah. Apparently, the families he talked to didn't think

giving their daughter to him was worth it." Luciano tried to hold his laugh in but was unsuccessful, which caused Gambino to laugh as Gotti sucked his teeth and grumbled under his breath. "Aw hell. You got me on speakerphone?"

"I do," Gambino answered through his laugh.

"Look, young blood, it was the hoing around. That might work for the average drug dealers or these other niggas in the streets, but you were born into an old school mafia family with a small amount of rules... but they value them above all. You don't rat, you don't cheat or sleep with a made man's wife, and you don't hurt women or children. Everything else can be justified."

A somber expression covered Gambino's face as he thought about his affair with Valerie. If he was anyone else, that would have ended in death. Back then, he knew his father wouldn't allow that and he took advantage. Thankfully, Cory never told him. It didn't matter how Gambino expressed his regret over the years, it was an act that Cory had forgiven but never threw into the sea of forgetfulness.

"Well, I'm acting right now," Gotti said. "I ain't saying I want an arranged marriage, but I know some of my actions have made us look bad as a whole." He shrugged. "I'm chilling."

"Good," Cory said. "Now... there were five families Samson was considering. When he got it to three a year ago, that's when the talks started to get serious. He ended up pulling out for Gotti and Luciano about three months ago. With him preparing to retire, his focus was only on you, Bino."

Gambino asked, "Did any of the families take the news poorly?"

"Poorly enough to be responsible for the bomb?"

Gambino nodded as if Cory could see him. "Yeah."

"I can't say. I can say they were upset. Joining us and the commission would have been profitable for them and us. However, the bomb seemed more like competition or a warning than retaliation."

"What were the five families?" Luciano asked, and Gambino grabbed a pen and pad to write them down.

When Cory was done naming them, Gambino sat back in his seat and stared at it.

"Of the options, the Russian and Mexican cartels were the best choices. The Russians in Chicago were probably bringing in the most value because of their weapons and cybercrime profit. However, your father knew you were adamant about continuing to blacken your bloodline. He valued your opinion even though it was his choice. He didn't say it, but I feel like that's why he called it off."

A somber moment of silence passed before Gambino cleared his throat and sat up in his seat.

"Thank you. Can you and Lu get me intel on all five families? I want to start with the Russians and Mexicans. If they were closest to the finish line, I think it's fair to assume they were most upset by him changing his mind."

"Got you," Luciano said, and Cory agreed.

"Listen..." Gambino took the call off speakerphone and stepped out of the study. "I know nothing I can say can make up for what I did but—"

"Stop. It's done."

"Yeah, but that shit eats at me, Cory. I was fucked up back then, no excuse. I apologize for what I did to you."

Cory sighed into the receiver. "I know, son. You've grown a lot. What you did cut me deep. It hurt me more than Valerie. I didn't trust her, but I trusted you. I have forgiven you, and I still love you and care about you, but I can't act like I can handle you the same way. I also can't act like you haven't matured and changed. This isn't me saying things will magically get better between us, but if Kayla can let you back in, I'll try too."

"I can't express how much that means to me, OG."

"We'll talk."

"Love."

"Love."

After disconnecting the call, Gambino leaned against the wall. Hearing about the arranged marriages would give them even more people to look into. It felt like they were getting further away from the truth instead of closer to it. Gambino still believed it was an inside job. If he could find out who planted the bomb, there was no doubt in his mind that they'd lead him to who they were working with.

***

Several Hours Later

"Nah, there was more," Gambino muttered, going through the pictures and his father's log. He'd been up for hours after the meeting with his brothers and date with Kayla. Though Cory said Samson had stopped talks of arranged marriages, Gambino vaguely remembered him taking meetings up until his death with different families.

Their security guards recorded at all times and took photos of visitors at all locations. He'd had the security photos pulled of his father's meetings over the last three months at his restaurant. None of the men he'd met with were familiar to Gambino. In Samson's log, he had written in bold, cursive font:

Russian bratva—Bino.
Brazilian cartel—Lu.
Irish mafia princess—Gotti.

Massaging his beard, Gambino stared at his father's writing.

"I don't think you changed your mind. I think you wanted them to think you did because you knew we wanted black wives." Standing, he pressed his palms against the desk. "What were you up to, Pops? If these were the families you chose for us, why didn't you tell us? Were the other two families upset by the decision you made? Is that why they bombed us?"

Gambino picked the picture up of Samson shaking hands with Mexican cartel leader Santiago Martinez and Lorenzo Ricci, the current boss of a Sicilian mafia. After sending the pictures to Luciano, he told his brother he wanted all five families moved up to the top of the list. He'd need to speak with them personally to figure out what was going on with his father. After making a to-do list for himself to forward to his personal assistant and the associate he used for cartel matters, Gambino trudged to the bedroom, where he found a naked, sleeping Kayla.

After handling his hygiene, Gambino slipped into bed behind her. As he wrapped his arms around her, he released a content sigh. Ending his days with Kayla wasn't a right; it was a privilege. A privilege he didn't think he'd ever get again. He said a silent prayer of gratitude for their reunion before tossing the comforter over them both and drifting off to sleep.

11

K ayla
    That Weekend

WORDS ESCAPED KAYLA AS SHE LOOKED OVER WHAT Gambino had done for her. A trail of red rose petals in the hall led to the guest bedroom next to their bedroom. Inside, the dimly lit room was full of specialists for an evening of pampering. Gambino had paid for her to get a massage, mani-pedi, and facial. When her pampering was over, she met him in their bedroom. It was filled with candles, curtain lights, rose petals, and candles of all shapes and sizes.

"Baby," she cooed as Gambino wrapped his arms around her.

"Do you like it?"

"I love it. Who did it?"

His chuckle was sexy as he turned her in his arms. "You saying I'm not capable of doing something romantic like this?"

"Yes, but I know you'll pay to make sure I have it."

Gambino laughed. "You damn right. Tonight's just the beginning. For the weekend, I belong to you."

"Ooh, I love the sound of that. What else do you have planned?"

"Shopping tomorrow, dinner at your favorite restaurant, and Sunday we'll take the jet wherever you want to go for a quick trip. I can't say how long we'll be able to stay, but I wanted to give you my undivided attention before..."

He silenced himself.

Kayla sighed and slid her hands down his chest as she licked her lips. "I know you don't tell me things about the business to protect me."

"That's correct. The less you know, the better."

"But... If you ever need to talk to me, I'm a great listener. And who knows, maybe I can offer fresh insight. I was raised in the lifestyle but not as deeply as you, so I see things with a different perspective."

"I would like to be able to talk to you about some things because you are my life partner, but we don't have to do that tonight, kitten."

"What better time? I know you're not into this kind of stuff, and I appreciate your effort. Let's sip some of that Hen, smoke some of your good ass weed, and talk."

"Mm," he moaned, gripping her ass. Gambino lowered to her ear and said, "If you want me to fuck you senseless, just say that."

"That really turned you on?" she asked through her laugh.

Gambino lowered her hand to his hardened dick. "Feel for yourself."

"Ooh. Mmm. I can't wait to taste and ride this."

She tugged Gambino toward the square table by the

floor to ceiling windows. He sat her on his lap like he always did when he missed her. While he rolled a blunt, she poured them both two fingers of Hennessy.

"So... How are things, Don Nahtahn?"

A wide grin spread Gambino's lips. "The transition has been smooth. Outside of the bomb we haven't had any issues."

"Do you have an idea of who did it?"

"We are looking into a few families who might have been upset about Pops changing his mind about joining our families in marriage. I have my associate setting up meetings for me to talk to them all, which is why I wanted to spend some time with you. I'll be bouncing from one city and country to the next to figure this shit out."

"Is there anything I can do to help or make this easier for you?"

Gambino eyed her as he considered her request. He took two puffs from the blunt, and she inhaled the smoke. As he handed her the blunt, he said, "The selfish part of me wants to ask you to come with me. The sane part of me wants you here where I know it will be safe."

"If you asked me to come, I would. It's not like I'm working or anything anyway."

"How do you feel about that?" he asked, accepting the blunt.

Kayla shrugged as she grabbed her glass and took a sip. "I don't want to work per se, but I have always wanted my own bookstore. Being here, having access to your dad's library, especially now that he's gone..." She sighed. "I don't know. It kind of makes me want it more."

"How are you handling his death? The focus is always on the immediate family when there's a loss, but I know you loved him too."

A choked sob escaped her before it turned into a humorless laugh. "I don't even think I've allowed myself to cry yet. I don't think I've really grieved him. I don't think I can."

"Why not?"

Kayla nibbled her bottom lip. "He meant a lot to me. Because of the bond we created over the years, but also because he was an extension of you. I guess I should say you were an extension of him." She smiled and looked away as his eyes watered. "He always accepted me and made me feel welcome. Like I was truly his daughter. Me and your mom are close but your dad..." She released a shaky breath as her tears threatened to pour. "He used to be so happy to see me and spend time with me. God... I think I'm about to cry."

They shared a quiet laugh as tears slid down her cheeks. Normally, he'd wipe them away. This time, Gambino let them flow freely.

"Keep talking. Let those tears come."

She nodded and pulled in a deep breath. "He said I was the first woman any of his sons brought around that felt like a daughter, and I think that's why we were so close. I mean, he took care of me like I was really your wife, Bino. When Papa first started talking about marrying me off, Daddy Samson was *livid*."

Gambino's brows wrinkled and head tilted as he squeezed her waist. "Around when was this?"

"Hmm... maybe a year ago."

"Did Pops mention wanting us to reconcile?"

"Well, he asked Papa if he thought it was possible. I told him no, but I found out recently that Papa told him he still believed there was hope for us."

Kayla watched him intently, as if she could literally see

his mind at work. Gambino chuckled and licked his lips before kissing hers.

"I need to speak with your father. I don't know for sure, but I think Pops planned to marry me off to some Russian woman and whatever he talked to your father about changed his mind. That's not to say he knew you and I would get to this point, but I find it amusing that when you started the process of finding your husband, Pops started pulling families out of his search. Maybe I'm overthinking it but—"

"No, don't doubt yourself. If you think there's a chance they are connected, definitely look into it."

Silence found them for a while before their conversation picked back up. They talked about their hopes, dreams, and plans for the future. Their likes and dislikes... how things had changed for them over the years. For hours, they talked and caught up, and Kayla's heart was light when their date was finally over. Then, Gambino made slow, passionate love to her until they both passed out.

<hr />

Saturday

BEING THE WIFE OF THE DON HAD ITS PERKS. THE PERK for that day was Gambino's version of shopping. He didn't just take her to the mall. He had it shut down for their arrival. For five hours straight, Kayla was able to bounce from one store to the next and not have to worry about crowds or lines. Anything she wanted, he got. Anything he wanted her to have, he got.

Their last stop in the mall was her favorite local jewelry store.

"Do you still want a proposal? Or can I just get you a ring?" he asked as they walked into the store hand in hand.

"Babe, after what you pulled last night, you can definitely put together a nice proposal. I deserve it."

"You know I can't say no to you. Let's pick your engagement and wedding rings, and I'll plan something."

"Wait, are you actually going to plan it, or get someone else to?"

His mouth dropped in shock before he laughed. "I feel like I should be offended by that question."

Kayla giggled, enjoying seeing the carefree and relaxed version of him. "I mean... you a gentle gangsta but when it comes to romance..."

"Aight, aight. I get it. Don't point out my flaws."

Her laughter increased. "It's literally the only thing that keeps you from being perfect. But you're perfect for me. I wouldn't trade you for anything or anyone else in this world."

A comfortable smile settled on Gambino's face as he cupped hers and kissed her sweetly. "You're making me soft, kitten. I'm enjoying myself too much with you."

"Is that really a bad thing?"

"Keep loving me. I'm brave enough to find out."

Kayla wrapped her arms around his neck and pulled him down to her for a kiss. The only reason she pulled away was to avoid their shopping trip ending for a quickie. She browsed every jewelry case in awe of the selection. Her final choices were a fifteen carat emerald cut white diamond and an eight carat emerald cut purple diamond... because that was her favorite color.

When Pierre slid the total over casually, her eyes ballooned at the price—fifteen million. Gambino didn't blink as he snapped his fingers. One of the guards that had been following them set three duffel bags on the display case.

Kayla grabbed his wrist and pulled him to the side.

"Baby... Are you sure?" she whispered. "That's a lot of money for two rings."

His expression hardened before he smiled and stroked his tie. "Don't ever question me about what I do for you. If you wanted a star, I'd find a way to wrangle one down and bring it back to you."

Leaving her speechless, Gambino placed a quick peck against her lips before heading back to the counter to finalize the transaction.

Sunday

"Ah!" Kayla immediately burst into tears. "You tricked me."

Gambino grinned as he held her hand and kept her from taking backward steps away from him. While she believed it would take time for his proposal, he already had something up his sleeve. Since they weren't sure if Gambino would have to abruptly return home, they elected not to leave the country. They went to one of her favorite resorts in California.

On the private beach, a large heart was shaped out of red roses. Large candles were scattered in between. As Gambino led her inside of the heart, Kayla wiped her tears. Soft music played from a keyboardist, and when she realized he was playing "Let's Get Married" by Jagged Edge, she laughed.

"Oh yeah, you definitely planned this," she teased, getting a laugh out of Gambino too.

"I did. What do you think?" he asked, expression turning serious as he held both of her hands in the center of the heart.

"I think it's perfect," she almost whispered before sniffling and fighting back more tears.

Gambino released a shaky breath. "I know this is supposed to be for the betterment of our families... an arranged marriage... a business arrangement... but it means more than that to me, kitten. I don't take this second chance lightly. I've always been in love with you, and if you give me the chance, I want to spend the rest of our lives showering you with the healthy love you deserve." As he pulled the engagement ring out of his pocket, he kneeled. "Kayla Lattimore, will you do me the highest honor of becoming my wife? Will you marry me, kitten?"

It was a moment Kayla thought would never come. Her head nodded adamantly before she burst into a fit of giggles.

"Yes, Gambino. I will marry you."

He tugged his bottom lip into his mouth. A short chuckle escaped him as he hung his head, then his watery eyes lifted toward the sky. He warmed her heart when he whispered a quick thanks to God before slipping the ring onto her finger. Then, he stood and enveloped her in a warm embrace. As their lips connected for a kiss, Kayla was convinced, nothing would bring her more joy than this.

After the proposal, they had a sunset champagne and prix fixe romantic dinner, and Kayla smiled and blushed the whole time.

"You not having second thoughts, are you?" Gambino asked, opening the door to their suite. "You've been cheesing but quiet as hell."

"Not at all. I'm in shock. I can't believe we're engaged. I'm really happy."

"Good."

"Are you happy too?" she asked sweetly, kicking her shoes off at the door.

"Happier than I've been my whole life. C'mere." Gambino pulled her close, connecting his lips with hers.

They made quick work of removing each other's clothes. Then, he carried her to bed. She was confused when Gambino left her, but that confusion was erased when he pull a black toiletry bag from his bag. One by one, he pulled out one delicately wrapped sex toy after another. Kayla's arousal increased her heart rate. By the time he made his way between her legs with the rose vibrator, her breathing was ragged, and her pussy was dripping wet.

Briefly, Gambino returned his lips to hers, but he pulled away to spread her legs and suck her clit into the rose. Her body instantly locked as she bit down on her bottom lip. His fingers went from one nipple to the other as he pleasured her. In less than two minutes, her back was arching off the bed, and she grunted as she came.

"Why you being quiet?" he asked, pulling the rose off.

"I don't want anyone to hear us."

"Fuck them. Focus on me." He put the rose back, higher on her clit that time, and she cried out as her legs locked. "Focus on how good I'm making this pussy feel."

"Oh my... hmm..."

Kayla's toes curled as she came again. "That's it. Get yours. Cum for daddy, kitten."

"Ooh... ooh shit!"

Gambino lowered the rose, positioning it at the hood of her clit. Her moans grew loud as she squirted against it and his arm. She pushed him away, clit tender and throbbing.

Choppy breaths escaped her as he tossed the rose and pulled her underneath him.

"Baby, I—" Her hand went to her pussy, but he swatted it away.

"Move that hand and let me get this pussy." Her mouth hung open as he filled her. "You gon' take this dick for me?" he asked against her ear, voice low and hushed compared to the dominate tone he usually used.

"Yesss, Bino. Make me take it."

Gambino stretched her arms over her head and pinned her hands to the bed as he stroked her. His pace increased as he methodically stroked her. Kayla wrapped her fingers around his, eyes rolling into the back of her head from the dizzying pleasure he was providing.

"I'm about to cum again," she warned, feeling that tingle spread up her spine.

"Who do you belong to?"

"Gambino," she moaned.

"And who's making this pussy cum?"

"G-Gambino!" she chanted over and over again as she convulsed underneath him.

"Mm... I'll never get tired of hearing you moan my name. Or watching your pretty ass cum. Look at those eyes. You're so fuckin' *beautiful*, Kayla. And you're all mine? Damn. I'm a lucky man."

His words combined with his strokes sent her over the edge. All it took was two circles of his thumb against her clit and she was cumming again. Needing to give her pussy a break from the pleasurable assault, Kayla pushed him out of her and laid him flat on his back. Her mouth went to work on his dick, licking her essence off and sucking until he came.

Gambino returned the oral favor before he put the dildo

and rabbit to use. By the time they were done, the bed was soaking wet, she was sprawled out on the couch, and Gambino was calling down to the lobby to see about new sheets... or a new suite, because he knew she'd be knocked out soon.

12

G ambino

"Surprise!"

"Oh my God!" Kayla yelled, jumping up and down.

Though Gambino wanted the proposal to be intimate, he planned a surprise party to celebrate their engagement when they arrived home. Not just so their loved ones would be able to help them celebrate the permanency of their love, but also so the other four families in the commission would know he was honoring his word to marry now that he was the don.

"You thought of everything, baby. Thank you!"

Kayla gave him a quick kiss before scurrying toward her parents and family. She didn't have many friends, but she hung with a few wives and daughters within several of the mafia families. His fiancée had always been the kind of woman who preferred the company of characters in books over human interaction, and that was what made having her attention mean so much when it was given.

"Congratulations, brotha. I'm proud of you," Luciano said, extending his hand for Gambino to shake.

"Do right by my sister, or I will hurt you, and that's on Pops," Gotti warned before shaking his brother's hand, and Gambino knew his baby brother was serious.

"I have no intentions of hurting my wife again. Trust me, I learned my lesson."

Luciano's eyes shifted before he said, "I hate to bring this to you right now, but it can't wait."

"Follow me to the study."

After hugging Delilah and shaking Bernie's hand, Gambino led his brothers upstairs to the study. Luciano wasted no time speaking as soon as the door closed behind them.

"You were right. It was an inside job."

He pulled his phone out, swiped a few times, then handed it to Gambino.

Gambino stared at the picture of the man and tried to recognize his face but came up short.

"He works for us?" Gambino confirmed.

"Yeah, and has been for the past five years."

"Clearly he was loyal, so what happened?"

"We have him in the dungeon now, but he ain't speaking. I had my hacker do some research and we do know he has a daughter who's sick. I don't know if whoever he planted the bomb for knew that and offered him money or medical treatment or what, but that's all we've come up with so far."

Gambino's head bobbed as he handed Luciano his phone. "I want answers. Tonight. Do whatever you have to do to him or his family to get them. And when you get them, you know what to do."

"I'm on it."

They left the study just as quickly as they'd entered. Though Gambino tried to return to the relaxed version of himself that he'd been while they were out of town, that was easier said than done. Now that they had the man who'd planted the bomb, he needed answers, and he wouldn't be able to rest until he found out who was responsible.

After the Party

"I APPRECIATE YOU STAYING BEHIND," GAMBINO SAID, offering Bernie a cigar.

"Of course. You looked like you had something on your mind all evening."

"It was that obvious?"

Bernie chuckled with a nod. "Probably not to everyone else, but I know what it looks like to be in deep thought over this shit. What's going on?"

Gambino pushed the ash tray that was on the table in the study further in Bernie's direction.

"Did you and my father discuss marriage between me and Kayla before he passed?"

"We did." Bernie took a pull from the cigar and sat up in his seat, resting his forearms on his thighs. "It was about a year ago. I wanted to start looking into families and of course you were at the top of my list. Even though things ended badly between you and Kayla all those years ago, I knew she still loved you. He asked me if I believed she was willing to give marriage with you a chance, and I told him I'd talk to her about it."

"She told me that. That she told you no."

"She did." Bernie smiled. "But I know my daughter. I knew that was coming from a place of hurt. Hurt that had been hiding and burying the love she had for you over the years. I assured your father if given the chance that you two could find your way back to each other. He told me to vet other families but keep you all in mind."

"Did that change? How'd you end up asking for permission to join the Yancy family?"

Bernie exhaled a hard breath. "Your father confided in me about his choices for you. He said that he didn't want to bring them to you because he knew you wouldn't approve. That you wanted a black wife and the options he had were not black. I told him if he felt they were the best options you'd agree but if he could just wait a little longer that I would try to convince Kayla to give you another chance." He paused. "About four months ago, we came to an agreement. Once he had his retirement plan completed, we'd talk to the both of you about getting married. By that point, something had happened with the Russians that made them unfavorable in your father's sight, and the Mexican cartel had just started a war with another family in Mexico City. He didn't want to take that risk. He told both families he had changed his mind but that he'd reach out if things changed."

"How did they take the news?"

"With the war going on, Santiago didn't care. Igor, however, did. He was banking on your family being his in here in the South. Your father didn't seem worried about Igor's anger, but he did mention that he blew up during the meeting and had to be pulled out."

"Why in the fuck didn't he mention any of this to me?"

"He didn't want you to know about his plans for you and Kayla just yet." His expression turned solemn. "When he died, I felt like that was it. Like the two of you and your future together had been buried right along with him. So when you told me y'all had started talking after the funeral, it was like Samson was working behind the scenes on your behalf."

Gambino ran his fingers down the corners of his mouth. "Thank you for sharing this with me... and for trusting me with your daughter again."

"You're welcome, but may I ask where this is coming from?"

"I think the Russians were responsible for the bombing. I don't have proof, but the more information I get, the stronger I feel that in my gut."

Bernie's mouth twisted to the side as he shook his head. "The Russians are ruthless and brutal, Bino. They do not tolerate disloyalty, and they don't play about family. It wouldn't surprise me if they did the bomb because they felt your father betrayed them by calling off the marriage. I just don't understand why they'd make their move after he died instead of within the months before."

"I don't know, but I'm damn sure about to find out."

13

G ambino

NEARING THE END OF HIS LIFE, JEREMY'S HEAD
bobbed. He was too weak to lift it as blood leaked from
several holes and gashes in his body. He'd die regardless, but
his answers over the next few seconds would determine
what Gambino ordered to have done to his family—if
anything.

Gambino gripped Jeremy's jaw and he groaned. Forcing
him to look at the picture of the Russian brigadier, Gambino
asked, "Is this who you were working for?"

The man was large with strong features, had blond hair,
and rocked the signature bratva tattoo on his hand. He was
seen entering Jeremy's girlfriend's nail shop with a black
bag and coming out empty handed. Shortly after, Jeremy
left holding that same bag. He had it when he went to the

Nahtahn warehouse the night of the bomb, but a few minutes later, he briskly walked out without it.

"It would be a shame for you to have crossed us for your family just for them all to die with you."

"N-no," Jeremy groaned, head bobbing like a figurine on a car dashboard. "Don't hurt my family. Please."

"Then tell me what I need to know."

Jeremy's eyes closed as he pulled in a deep breath. "That's him. Boris. He came to me and offered more than enough for my daughter's medical bills if I delivered that bag to the warehouse."

"Did he say why?"

His head shook. "No." Jeremy grimaced before releasing a low, "Argh."

"Why didn't you come to us if you needed help with your daughter?"

With flaring nostrils, Jeremy widened his eyes as much as he could to look into Gambino's. "Too proud. I didn't ask them. They offered."

Gambino chuckled as he stood. "Do you know anything else? Do they plan to do another attack?"

"I don't know. I had no way to contact them, and they didn't let me in on anything. Not even what was in the bag. They approached me one day with half a million dollars, pulled up to my girl's shop with the bag, then came back the next morning with the rest of the money. I haven't heard from them since."

Gambino's head bobbed once as he stared at Jeremy. "Alright." His eyes shifted toward Luciano. Though he was technically the underboss, being an enforcer was still in his blood. It was in both their blood. However, Gambino knew it was his role to give orders now, not execute them. So as much as he wanted to get his hands dirty, he refrained. Instead, he told Luciano, "Put 'em down," before leaving the warehouse.

"His family?" Luciano confirmed.

"P-please!" Jeremy yelled weakly before it turned into a sob.

His head shook and Luciano received the directive, but he remained silent, wanting Jeremy to suffer as much as he could before his death.

ONCE JEREMY WAS TAKEN CARE OF, THE NAHTAHN hacker, Cole, was able to track Igor and Boris down in Chicago. With Cory's insistence, Gambino agreed to stay behind and spend the day with his fiancée. He put a team together that his brothers and cousins would lead, and he would watch sporadically via drone.

"I want as many or more of their men gone as the ones we lost," Gambino made clear. "Don't come back home until that's taken care of. Make sure they learn we ain't *nothing* to fuck with."

He shook hands with his brothers and sent them away before going home, in need of a distraction.

"Where's my wife?" Gambino asked, leaving the library.

"Last I saw her, she was in the sunroom," Braxton answered, heading down the opposite end of the hall, focused on whatever paperwork he was looking at.

Gambino headed toward the sunroom, and his body instantly warmed at the heat that radiated from it. It was early February, and it didn't start to feel like winter in

Tennessee until January and February. Thankfully, it wouldn't last for too long, because he was ready to see Kayla on the beach. For now, their heated indoor pool would have to do.

"Kitten," he called softly, and she sat up instantly. Setting her book on the chair next to her, Kayla smiled. She reached her arms out for him, and Gambino wasted no time picking her up.

"Where are we going?"

"Anywhere you want," he answered as he carried her out of the room.

"You know what I have a taste for?"

"What?"

"Fried buffalo fish from *Lamar's Fish Shack*."

"That's a very specific request, kitten."

Lamar's Fish Shack was in the hood of Rose Valley Hills. It was also the first place Gambino took Kayla years ago. During that time in his life, he was a rebellious nineteen year old who wanted nothing to do with the wealth and opulence that came from being a part of the Nahtahn Cartel. Saying he had an identity crisis at that point in his life would be an understatement. He was trained to be lethal and powerful, yet his surroundings of wealth and seclusion gave the opposite vibe.

It was hard for him to maintain friendships with anyone outside of the organization because they couldn't understand the lifestyle and all that went along with it. For quite some time, Gambino tried to find his place with street niggas who didn't live the same code he did, and that led to more harm than good. He was at war with the principles his father and Cory were instilling into him and his brothers versus what he was learning in the streets.

Then, he met Kayla Lattimore. His father told him one day she'd be his wife. That they would help take the Nahtahn Cartel to new heights. And that responsibility, for a teenager, was too much. And so... he began to rebel.

But that night at *Lamar's Fish Shack*... that night he and Kayla came to an agreement. If their fathers were going to force them into an arranged marriage they'd do it their way —as friends. That night, they got to know each other. They talked for hours. Whether Gambino wanted to admit it or not, that was the night he fell in love. After their meal, they went to the boardwalk and spent the rest of their evening on the beach. He'd been obsessed with her ever since.

"I've been thinking about our path a lot," Kayla confessed as he put her feet on the carpeted floor of their bedroom. "Though I hate how things ended, I think that break was for the best. Had we stayed together for the past eight years, I don't know how our bond would be now. We had a lot of growing up to do, you know? You've changed a lot, and I have too. I like these versions of us."

"I'm glad to hear you say that, and I think it would be okay to take a trip down memory lane. That neighborhood has gotten worse, though, so stay close."

"Oh, I'm not worried at all. I'll be with the don."

Her wide smile and teasing tone as she wrapped her arms around him made Gambino's heart swell.

"That's true, but young niggas out that way don't care who you are. I don't want to have to get in that element in front of you, so stay at my side, and stay alert."

"Yes, daddy."

"Cut that out before we don't leave this room," Gambino warned before wrapping his hand around her neck and kissing her. Pressing his dick against her, he circled his arm around her. Kayla released a content sigh as she stroked it. "Get dressed, Kayla. Now."

Her cackle made his heart skip a beat as she walked away. Like back in the day, she had a way of making him feel light when he was surrounded by darkness. She made his stomach flutter, but he refused to say with butterflies. Whatever it was, they only flew around with her.

Once she was dressed in a sweatsuit and heels, Gambino dressed down as well, and he opted to cruise around the city with his lady in her favorite car from his collection—the Rolls-Royce Phantom. He wanted security but also the intimacy of alone time with her, so he drove and had a two man security team follow behind.

Instead of going straight to *Lamar's*, they stopped and grabbed a bottle of tequila since that was what she had a taste for. They smoked and took a few shots while talking about how they wanted their lives to play out. The amount of kids they wanted. How long Gambino planned to rule as the don. Their expectations from each other during this new stage of their lives and relationship. What other passions and desires they had. When she started to giggle a bit more, Gambino knew it was time to feed her. They left the park and headed to *Lamar's*, and thanks to Gambino's assistant, he was already expecting them.

Gambino parked in the back, and Lamar was waiting for them at the exit door. His grin was wide as they headed in his direction hand in hand. Gambino understood his excitement, seeing as Gambino and the Nahtahn Cartel were hood legends—celebrities in Rose Valley Hills. One mention of Gambino and Kayla being there would have the place packed for the next several months.

The men shook hands and Lamar kissed Kayla's before leading them to a table in the back of the restaurant, where

Gambino and the guards were able to watch everyone and all exits. He set his Glock 18 on the table, and its presence immediately caused a table of men to stop looking in their direction. The semiautomatic pistol was illegal and hard to come by, but everyone in his cartel had one.

"What can I get y'all?" Lamar asked, pulling a pencil from behind his ear and notepad from his waist. "I'm taking care of y'all personally."

Kayla's high had kicked in, so she had the munchies. Along with her desired buffalo fish, she got slaw, green beans, and spaghetti with Cajun fries and fried green tomatoes as her appetizer. Gambino knew she wouldn't eat all of that, so he added fried catfish and no additional appetizers, opting to share hers instead.

"I'm high as fuck," she announced before laughing and leaning into his side.

"I don't know why you thought you could handle rotating two blunts with me."

"I forgot what I was smoking. I could usually smoke three or four blunts and be fine, but your weed is so potent, and I'm not saying that to gas you, Bino. Y'all really offer high quality, potent weed. It genuinely doesn't take that much."

Her words stroked his ego as he wrapped his arm around her shoulders from the back and lay her on his chest. She kicked her feet up as her eyes lazily scanned the room. Gambino's eyes closed briefly as he enjoyed the Earth, Wind, & Fire that crooned in the background. Spending time with her was helping keep his mind off what his family was about to do in Chicago without him.

"I love you," he whispered against her ear before kissing it.

Kayla reached her arm back and cupped his neck,

holding him in place so she could turn and kiss his lips. "I love you."

"Thank you for being my wife. The world will be at your feet. Whatever you want, kitten, it's yours."

Her smile spread as she brushed her nose against his cheek. "I only want you."

"Maybe right now, but you know that ain't true."

She giggled. "Let me be romantic, babe."

"Do your shit, Kayla."

She laughed again as she shifted slightly against him. "This is perfect. I know we could go anywhere and do anything. I don't think I'm necessarily low maintenance, but I really am so content just being with you. Whether we do that here, at home, or in another country... I just want to be with you."

Gambino pushed her hair out of her face and cupped her cheek before kissing her. He didn't give a fuck about those looking. How love, to the wrong people, could be perceived as weakness. He was just grateful he had his kitten back.

Lamar quietly set their appetizers on the table, and the swiftness in which Kayla lifted from his chest tickled him, but he didn't call her out on it. Depending on if the food sobered her up or made her higher would determine their next move for the night.

They silently scarfed down their food. When they were done, she was ready to go to sleep, like he figured she would be. As they walked out the back, Lamar called his name.

"Take my wife to the car," Gambino said to the two guards.

He listened as Lamar expressed his grievances about the neighborhood. How the safety of its citizens was one of his biggest concerns. How a lot of young niggas who didn't understand the value of keeping their neighborhood a safe zone were causing a lot of gang wars, robberies, and senseless murders.

"Now don't get me wrong, I was wild back in the day," Lamar continued, "but we knew to do our dirt outside of our backyard. At the rate these hoodlums are going, the block will soon be condemned. It's already ranked the most unsafe neighborhood in Tennessee and the secret society is considering moving everyone out." Lamar paused and looked back at his restaurant. "If they gentrify our neighborhood, a lot of people are going to be displaced. A lot of businesses will be closed. I want them to understand if they pluck these people out, they won't do nothing but wreak havoc in other neighborhoods."

"Then what do you propose, OG?"

"Make this neighborhood safer and better. If I had the reach to get in some of those secret society meetings, I could have my voice heard, but I don't have that kind of pull."

"I hear you. I got a lot going on right now, but I'll consider what you're saying. Maybe I'll buy the block and ensure it isn't gentrified. After that, if the secret society isn't willing to invest in the community to make it safer—"

"Ooh wee, this is nice as fuck."

At the sound of an unfamiliar voice, Gambino turned his head toward the left. A frown covered his face at the sight of six men circling his car.

"We finna get this shit," another voice said.

His guards stood in front of the passenger door, but that didn't stop one of the men from opening the driver side door.

"I'm 'bout to hop inside."

"Keep them niggas over there."

At that point, all hell broke loose. Their attempt to steal the car was quickly denied. While one guard remained at the door to keep Kayla secured, the other reached for his piece and aimed, but it didn't matter, because Gambino was on top of it.

All six bodies fell backward as Gambino's bullets entered them. Their guns and knives flew out of their hands as their bodies hit the concrete.

Lamar had ducked for cover, but when Gambino lowered his gun, he returned to his side. "I'll wait until you leave to call the police. You know they won't be in a rush to come out here anyway."

Gambino couldn't ignore the sadness in his voice or in his eyes. This was *exactly* what Lamar was complaining about. Though Gambino believed him, seeing it unfold so quickly sobered him up and made him aware of just how serious the problem was. Kayla opened the door, and before she could make her way over to him, the guards barricaded her in front of the car.

"If y'all don't get your big asses out of my way!" she yelled, shoving Robert's chest. "Move so I can get to my husband!"

Gambino's head hung as he shoved his hands in his sweats and walked in her direction.

"I'm fine, kitten," he assured her, motioning with his head for the guards to go to their car.

Kayla jogged and closed the space between them, hopping into his arms. She held his face in place as she kissed him.

"It happened so fast. They were bold as hell. Are you okay?" she checked.

"I'm good. Are *you* okay?"

"Mhm. I knew you'd protect me. I don't trust anyone with my life the way I trust you."

His steps faltered. "You mean that shit?"

"I do."

Gambino stepped over two bodies as the guards' gloved hands moved them away from the Rolls-Royce. He opened the back door and put her inside. Once he was seated comfortably, Kayla pushed his sweats down and took his hardened dick into her mouth.

"Fuck," he groaned, gripping the back of her head.

The thought of her being aroused after watching him lay bodies down made his dick harder than it had ever been. His stomach clenched when she held his balls against his shaft and licked and sucked both at the same time. He'd never cum so quick in his life. Kayla pushed her sweats and panties down before straddling him. As she rode him, he lifted her hoodie and sucked each nipple. Her back arched as she moaned and rocked against him.

Gambino didn't bother with dirty talk. He was too consumed by the pleasure being inside of her provided. He did, however, tell her, "Turn that ass around. Let me see it while you ride this dick," after she came.

Kayla did as she was told, pressing the light and illuminating the car before sliding back down on his saturated dick.

"Mm," he moaned, sliding down further in his seat.

It seemed the police were closer than Lamar gave them credit for, because he heard the sirens before he saw the flashing blue and white lights. His eyes trained on the three police cars as they entered the parking lot, but Gambino didn't give a fuck.

"Faster," he commanded, smacking her ass.

Kayla whimpered and granted his request. His head

rested against the seat as the lights bounced against the car. Gambino wrapped one arm around her neck while the other reached around her waist. As he held her close, he massaged her clit.

"Yesss, baby. That feels so good. I'm about to cum again."

"I know, kitten. I feel that shit. Go ahead and cum."

Her body trembled against him and walls pulsed as she did just that. Seconds later, Gambino erupted inside of her. He held her close as they composed themselves. When he was ready to pull out, Gambino kissed her shoulder and rubbed her ass. She lifted and they pulled their garments up. Gambino opened the door, casually holding her hand to help her out. All guns were trained on them as police yelled for them to lift their hands. Ignoring them, Gambino opened the passenger door and told Kayla, "Get in, kitten."

His eyes locked with the lead detective, who immediately ordered the police officers to stand down when he recognized him. As Gambino headed to his side of the car, he heard the detective order one of them to escort the don home. No questions needed to be asked. No stories needed to be told. What happened there that night would be buried, and the money the Nahtahns funneled through the police department would make sure of it.

1:00 AM

THE SOUND OF VIBRATING JOLTED GAMBINO OUT OF HIS sleep. He grabbed his phone and shuffled out of bed. When he answered the call, his cousin told him to log in to see what was happening on the drone. Gambino waited until he was in the study to log in. Pride filled him as he watched the drone hover over his men while they conquered everyone in the garage. Though he was filled with satisfaction, Gambino knew there was a chance the retaliation wasn't ending what the Russians started.

In fact, something told him it was just the beginning.

14

K ayla
A Few Days before Valentine's Day

CLAIRE WRAPPED HER ARM AROUND KAYLA'S. THEY'D spent the day together on Gambino's dime. He paid for a four hour spa experience, shopping, and lunch at Claire's favorite sushi restaurant. As they strolled down Main Street, Claire said, "Thank you for keeping an old lady company."

"You know I love spending time with you. How are things with your sister?"

Claire groaned, causing Kayla to giggle. "She's driving me crazy. She's so particular. I think I want to move out."

"Well, you know you can move back in with us. There's no reason for us to have all that space."

"Bino said the same thing. I love having the cove with our family there, but I think I'm ready for something of my own. Maybe the small mother-in-law suite behind Gotti's home."

"That would be nice."

"How are things with your parents?"

"Good. Mommy is finally back to herself. That flu spell really had her down for a while. She's gone back to teaching. Papa's been working like crazy in preparation for the changes after Bino and I get married."

"How are you feeling about that now that time has passed? And when can I expect my first grandbaby?"

Kayla gushed as they walked into her favorite bookstore —*Booked and Brewed*—that also had a coffee shop.

"I feel confident. The more we talk and spend time together, the more I love him. As far as the baby... I'm on birth control, but Bino wants me to get off after the wedding."

"Which will be..." Claire prodded, nudging Kayla's shoulder softly.

"This fall or next. I don't have any other details yet. It will have to be grand, that I know for sure."

"I'm excited. Bino has had a light in his eyes because of you. He smiles unintentionally, and I know it's because he's thinking of you. I feared becoming don would harden my son even more, but loving you, having you, it balances him out."

Kayla was filled with pride at the sound of her future mother-in-law's words. "I battled with letting him in or not. I felt stupid going back to a man that cheated on me, but Bino's truly not that man. I feel so safe with him, Mama Claire. In all ways. I'm just really happy we got a second chance."

"Aww, you're going to make me cry."

Kayla laughed lightly as Claire pulled her in for a hug.

When they released each other, they grabbed two mugs of coffee and sipped slowly before buying a few books. When they headed out, Robert asked her if they wanted to continue to walk, or if they were ready to head back home. Ready for a nap, Kayla told him they could head home. As they neared the town car, everything happened in a blur.

One minute, Robert was opening the door for them, and the next, he was shoving Kayla into the car as gunfire rang out. A bullet pierced his shoulder, but that didn't stop him from tossing Claire into the car, closing the door, and returning fire. Their driver swerved onto the street, and Kayla yelled for him to go to the nearest hospital at the sight of blood leaking from Claire's chest.

"No, no, no, no, no, no, no," she muttered, pressing Claire's chest as it leaked. "Keep your eyes open, Mama. Stay with me."

Claire gasped for air as she gripped Kayla's wrist. "M-my babies..."

"You'll see them at the hospital. Just keep your eyes open and stay with me."

Claire's eyes fluttered as tears poured from Kayla's. She prayed harder than she ever had for God to spare Claire's life. Gambino had *just* lost his father on New Year's Eve.

How would he handle losing his mother now?

At the Hospital

KAYLA PACED THE WAITING ROOM. THE DOCTORS refused to give her any updates on Claire. They didn't care that she was Gambino's fiancée. Since they weren't married yet, they couldn't release any information. She was so confused and unsure if it was a random drive-by or if they'd been targeted.

"Kayla," Luciano barked, gaining her attention.

Her heart settled at the sight of all three brothers charging down the hall. Gambino ended the phone call he was on and pressed his way through his brothers to get to her. He looked her over intently as Luciano asked what happened. When she was done, Gambino hugged her as Gotti asked for an update on their mother.

"They wouldn't tell me anything. They said I wasn't family since we aren't married yet. I should have lied but I wasn't thinking."

Gambino's nostrils flared as he stormed over to the nurse's station. "Aye. Bring me Claire Nahtahn's doctors... now." Before she could walk away, Gambino grabbed the neck of her shirt and pulled her close. She yelped when her body connected with the desk.

"Gambino," Kayla pleaded softly.

He looked down at Kayla and loosened his grip on the woman. "This woman is my wife," he made clear. "Damn what a piece of paper says. You give her any and all updates when me and my brothers are not here. Do you fuckin' understand me?"

"Y-yes, sir," she agreed quickly, body trembling as she looked toward Kayla for help.

Kayla covered Gambino's hand with hers and gently pulled it off the nurse, who scurried away quickly. When she returned with a doctor pulling a mask from his face, Kayla took Gambino's hand into hers.

"You all are Mrs. Nahtahn's sons," he confirmed.

"And this is her daughter," Gotti said.

"Whatever you gotta tell us, you can tell her," Luciano added.

The doctor rolled on his heels and swallowed hard as his expression softened. "Unfortunately, there won't be any other updates to give."

"What does that mean?" Gambino asked, tightening his grip on Kayla's hand.

"I'm so sorry. We did everything we could, but Mrs. Nahtahn succumbed to her injuries."

"W-what?" Luciano stuttered as Gambino's body swayed.

"She's gone?" Gambino confirmed.

"No!" Gotti roared, grabbing the doctor by his neck and smashing his fist against his face. "Bring her the fuck *back*!"

By the third hit, the doctor was unconscious. It took both brothers to pull a sobbing Gotti off the doctor. As they carried him out, Gambino yelled for Kayla to sit with their mother while they got him under control. Her head shifted from the left to the right. Gotti's piercing pleas for them to bring his mother back... Luciano's silent tears... Gambino's distant gaze.

Slow, small steps led her to Claire's room. Her eyes focused on her still, lifeless body. Clutching Claire's cheek, Kayla's head shook as she prayed for peace to consume her soul.

"God, what have they done?" she cried. "Taking her... Her sons are about to tear this city *apart*."

15

G ambino
After the Funeral

THE VOICES OF THOSE AROUND HIM WERE GOING IN ONE ear and out of the other. At thirty-years-old, Gambino felt like an orphan. He'd been like a zombie, not present mentally and emotionally. Luciano had been acting out the orders Gambino barely had the consciousness to give. And Gotti? Gotti had been on a fucking *rampage*. If he wasn't fucking he was fighting and shooting... and he'd been doing a lot of both.

Kayla had been trying her hardest to reach each brother. She'd gotten them to agree to stay at the estate. Luciano was never home, and Gotti was drunk when he was there. Gambino didn't have the luxury of using a vice to numb himself, because for the sake of the cartel, he had to be alert. He'd been battling his heart and mind since his mother was killed, and grief was winning.

Worse, Kayla had been suffering with survivor's guilt, and Gambino could barely tend to her because of his own issues. Every night, she cried and asked God why He spared her instead of Claire. Thankfully, her parents were temporarily staying at the estate too, because as much as he wanted to be the strong safety net she expected him to be, he couldn't. He kept telling himself after the funeral he'd be more present. And Kayla assured him she was okay. That he needed to focus on himself and the cartel. That she could handle her grief alone and still hold space for his.

That was what she was doing now. Her grip on his hand was firm as one person after the next came up to the three brothers to offer their condolences. Cory stepped forward, and with a sympathetic gaze told them, "They're in the room. All weapons have been confiscated."

Gambino dropped a kiss to Kayla's forehead. "After this, we can leave."

"Okay, baby."

She rubbed Gotti's back and he gave her a kiss on her temple, and Luciano did the same.

The brothers made their way into the meeting room of the church. His eyes shifted from Boris to his daughter Inessa. Apparently, it wasn't Igor, the pakhan, who sent the order to bomb their warehouse. It was his second in command, Boris. Igor's children had been killed, and the only one still living was a son in prison. They were going to use Boris's daughter to bring the families together, and in exchange, Boris would be guaranteed Igor's place when he retired.

When Boris found out the marriage wouldn't happen, he was upset, because that meant his position was no longer guaranteed. His response? Going after the person he held responsible—Gambino. To him, Gambino had rejected his daughter, and because of that, he had to be punished. Boris's plan was to attack his product and then his family. Out of respect for Samson, he didn't bother him. But when he heard Gambino was getting married after the funeral, his rage overflowed. Boris regretted not striking soon, and he vowed to not make that mistake again. So, when his men had clear shots at Claire, he ordered them to take it.

Kayla and Gambino's brothers were next on his list, but he reached out to Igor for peace. Boris thought that meant he'd be safe at the meeting.

Gambino's jaw clenched as he looked at Boris. Flashes of his mother's lifeless body from minutes earlier entered his mind. He'd brought them there to talk and make sure they understood the gravity of what they'd done. He wanted Boris to see his daughter's soul leave her body before his did the same. They were supposed to be taken from the church and tortured first. All of that left Gambino's mind. Before he could stop himself, he pulled his Glock and sent bullets through both their skulls.

"In the church, bruh?" Luciano taunted with a small grin.

"The bible does say vengeance is the Lord's," Gotti said, smiling for the first time since their mother was killed.

"God be busy. It was my pleasure to handle this one," Gambino said.

As they left the meeting room, he told Cory to have the cleanup crew dispose of the bodies as he dialed Igor's number.

"Yeah?" Igor grunted.

"It's done."

"Boris had to go. He disobeyed a direct order to stand down. Thank you for handling that for me."

"And to confirm..."

"We're ghosts. You'll never hear from us again. I do have a shipment being delivered to the warehouse as apologies for the bombing. Do with it what you will."

While Gambino appreciated the gesture, he'd never push anyone's product but his own. As he stepped into the sanctuary, the pressure that had been on his chest seemed to start to lift. He had a lifetime left of grieving his parents but knowing the person responsible for the bombing and his mother's death was killed gave him peace. It cut his heart back on. A smile lifted the corners of his mouth at the sight of Kayla. Taking her into his arms, he kissed her sweetly.

"Let's go home, kitten."

Three Weeks Later

THE FOG HAD LIFTED ENOUGH FOR GAMBINO TO FEEL comfortable taking Kayla out of the country to celebrate Valentine's Day since it was clouded by their grief. Business was running smoothly, and though Gambino missed his parents daily, he also fought to be present for who was still living. Kayla and his brothers were at the top of that list. Claire's death softened Cory's heart toward him. The two had been speaking daily, and Gambino appreciated it.

On their way to the airport, Gambino stopped by the commercial building he'd purchased for Kayla's bookstore. It was a small gesture to show her that he not only believed in her but appreciated her being in his life. Being by his side.

She was in her own world as he got out of the Maserati and walked over to her side, not looking up until he opened her door.

"We're at the airport already?"

Gambino chuckled as he shook his head. "No. I made a pit stop."

Holding Kayla's hand, he led her to the door of the four-thousand square feet space. "What's this?" she asked.

"Hmm... I don't know. What did you plan to call your bookstore?"

With a gasp, she dropped his hand and looked at him with wide, expressive eyes.

"Gambino... baby..." She twirled and looked around the empty space. "You bought this for me?"

"I did. Go inside and have a look. Thirty minutes, then we have to leave."

"Ah! I'm so excited!"

She ran toward the door then turned and ran into his arms. His hearty laughter filled her ear as he picked her up and held her close.

"Thank you, thank you, thank you. I love you!"

"And I love you more."

That was true.

Hell, Gambino was starting to think he loved Kayla more than he loved himself, and he couldn't *wait* until she officially became his wife.

The Present

16

G otti Nahtahn
    One Year Later

THE BROTHERS WERE IN PUERTO VALLARTA FOR A
weeklong vacation after checking on their weed farms in
Guadalajara and Mexico City. They'd return home after
checking in on their product in Cuba. Since the Nahtahn
Cartel operated as suppliers for several drug rings and
gangs, they made sure they had enough product to never
run out of supply. To do that, they grew their weed in
Memphis, Chicago, Miami, Las Vegas, Guadalajara,
Mexico City, and Cuba. That also allowed them to supply
their customers without having to send the product long
distances.

As they had dinner at Noroc, Gambino shifted the
conversation to a serious matter. It was one of their
favorite restaurants when they were in Puerto Vallarta.
Gotti loved the beaches there and the nightlife. Like

Vegas, he'd go there and party for days straight with no sleep.

"Things with Igor are secured," Gambino said. "He respects me honoring my word and not going after any more of his people after what Boris did."

"Is he willing to still be our arms dealer?" Luciano checked.

"Yes, if we supply him. Apparently he's tried our product and concedes that it's better than what he's getting from his current supplier. I'm cool with that."

"I mean... he's not just good for weapons," Gotti said. "His cybercrime team has access to billions. I know we were against working with him in the beginning, but Pops saw his value clearly. You're with sis now, but I think we should still consider doing more business with him."

"Yeah, but are we willing to dabble in that shit?" Luciano questioned. "All money ain't good money. We don't do trafficking of any kind. No kidnappings. No fraud."

Gotti chuckled with a shake of his head. "Mobsters with morals. Right."

"Exactly," Gambino agreed. "And we ain't mobsters. Not by legal definition. We are a mafia cartel, but everything we do is with structure, honor, and decency. Even when we blow a nigga's head off." Gambino paused and took a sip of his whiskey. "With that being said, if we could find a way to benefit from what they do digitally, I wouldn't be opposed to it."

"He just pulled off a bitcoin scam," Gotti shared. "He made ten million dollars holding the shit ransom. They paid him that to get their shit back. I don't see anything wrong with that."

Gambino's mouth twisted to the side as he considered his brother's words.

"I hate to admit it, but I don't either," Luciano replied. "Igor's known for his ransom racketeering. It's brought in millions. He doesn't always do the crime. He makes a hell of a lot of money just off the fear and thought of it being done. If no one actually gets hurt from it, maybe we should look into it."

"Besides, if the people he runs these scams on have millions and billions to pay, they won't miss what we take," Gotti added.

Gambino's head shook. "I would really have to think on that. It'll bring in money, but it goes against my principles. I've never taken anything from anyone. What we have, we built from the ground up. I'll think on it though. For real." Gambino shifted his attention to Gotti. "I have an assignment for you when we get back home."

"What is it?" Gotti asked.

"Now that Ma has been gone for a year now, her company has taken a hit. Of our legal establishments, hers means the most to me. I believe her workers have gotten sloppy because she isn't there anymore. We're losing major clients and not bringing new ones in. I want you to go in and get that shit together."

Gritting his teeth, Gotti sat back in his seat. He knocked back the rest of his vodka and ran his hand over his face.

"Big brotha, I respect your decision to sit me down from cartel matters, but it's been a year. How long is this shit supposed to last?"

"Depending on how you handle this, you can come back when you're done." Gambino sat up and lowered his tone. "*Nahtahn Designs* has been in our family for twenty years. That's Ma's legacy. I chose you because I know how close you were to her, and I figured this would help you with your grief. Outside of that, we clean a hell of a lot of money through there. If we're losing clients and our numbers are dropping, we won't be able to explain how we're bringing in the same amount at the end of the year. So even though you aren't in the field or warehouses with your teams, this job is just as serious. We've had no issues cleaning our money and getting on the IRS's radar. I'm expecting you to keep it like that."

With Gambino being willing to explain his reasoning, it made it easier for Gotti to agree. He had been struggling with grieving their mother. Though he'd gotten out of using drugs and alcohol or women to numb himself, his brothers complained that he wasn't processing his grief in a way that would allow him to release it. They feared one day he'd explode.

Maybe being in Claire's office would help him feel closer to her. It wasn't like it was outside of the norm of what he was doing back home anyway. Without being in control of their soldiers, the bulk of Gotti's days were spent checking in and handling affairs for their legal businesses. Though the task was boring compared to being in the streets, he took pride in helping keep their businesses on the right track. *Nahtahn Designs* would be no different.

"Aight, I'll give it about three months. Anything or anyone in particular you want me to look into?"

Gotti listened intently as Gambino gave him a thorough rundown of what he'd been hearing about. He also made it clear that he wanted Gotti to fire the current man in charge and anyone else who had a problem with him being there. After their conversation was over, they shifted back into relaxation mode before finding a club to spend the rest of their night in.

17

R ue
Two Weeks Later
Late February

RUE WALKED INSIDE OF *BOOKED & BREWED* FOR HER usual white chocolate mocha latte with caramel syrup. Unable to resist, she browsed the new arrival section to see if anything new would catch her eye. A low hum escaped her at the sight of the flyer that was in front of the books on the table. It was for the grand opening of a new black owned bookstore in Rose Valley Hills. Intrigued by what the new store would have to offer, she slipped it inside of her purse then went to the pickup counter for her latte. After chatting with the barista for a while, Rue headed out of the store and to the left for work.

Her penthouse apartment was in the heart of downtown Rose Valley Hills, making it easy for her to walk to work and anywhere else she needed to go. Where she couldn't walk, she used a town car, because she hated driving. Though she wouldn't have been able to afford the ten thousand dollar monthly rent on her salary, she used the monies she received from the payout after the bad car accident that increased her anxiety about driving to pay for it. If Rue could go back in time, she would have chosen not to be the target of a millionaire's drunk driving. However, the settlement had changed her life in ways she was still grateful for, teaching her how something bad could work for her good.

After the short five minute walk to *Nahtahn Designs*, Rue headed inside with a smile. Being at work was truly the highlight of her day. The only thing that would have made it better was a promotion, but unfortunately, she didn't see that happening any time soon. Now that Claire Nahtahn was gone, Raul Norman was her replacement, and though Rue could understand why he was CEO, that didn't make it an easier pill to swallow. She reminded herself often that she was an amazing designer, but that did nothing to dim her desire to be more.

As she made her way through the office, it was in complete chaos. At the sound of yelling coming from Raul's office next to hers, Rue quickly set her things on her desk and rushed over to see what was going on. People often mistook her small stature for weakness, but they learned quickly that she was nothing to fuck with.

"Get yo' shit, and get the fuck out," a man Rue didn't recognize ordered. His voice was stern and commanding. Still, that didn't stop Rue from charging over to him.

"I don't know if you realize it, but this is a place of business. Clients are already making their way inside. You need to lower your voice. In fact... Why don't you just shut the fuck up?"

18

G otti

"I DON'T KNOW IF YOU REALIZE IT, BUT THIS IS A PLACE of business. Clients are already making their way inside. You need to lower your voice. In fact... Why don't you just shut the fuck up?"

"Who the fuck said that shit?"

"Hey!" At the feel of a tiny hand shoving his shoulder, Gotti looked down. "I'm down here, asshole."

He was so focused on Raul that he didn't see the little fireball roll her way inside. That was a rare occurrence. Usually, Gotti was *always* aware of his surroundings. The longer he looked at her, the less disrespect he felt by her words. He wanted to question who the hell she thought she was to speak to him that way, but he couldn't help but notice how beautiful she was.

She had to be over a foot shorter than him. Her chest

poked out and nostrils flared with her determination. Whoever she was, she certainly didn't look like a threat or that she cursed for that matter.

"Aye, who the fuck you think you talking to?" Gotti asked, refusing to bow to anyone—especially a smurf—regardless of how beautiful that smurf was.

"You're the one causing this chaos, so I'm talking to you. Who the hell do you think you are to be telling the CEO to leave anyway?"

Sucking his teeth, Gotti cupped his hands together in the center of him before releasing a chuckle.

"I'm the new CEO of *Nahtahn Designs*. Now unless you want to be fired like him, you need to back your little ass up."

"The only person who would have the authority to fire me is Gambino Nahtahn, and seeing as he didn't make me aware of his arrival—"

"That's my brother, dummy," Gotti said, cutting Raul off. His head tilted, and Raul's eyes widened at the sight of the NC tattoo in the center of his neck. Every member of the cartel had the tattoo either on the side of their neck or on their wrists, but the brothers had them on the center of their necks.

"I-I... I'm s-so s-sorry," Raul scrambled. "I didn't know you were coming, Mr. Nahtahn. Had I known..."

"I don't give a fuck about all that shit," Gotti said with a huff as his irritation rose. "You need to get your shit and get the fuck out. Take yo' lil pit bull with you too." He looked down at the woman with a snarl as she crossed her arms and rolled her eyes. "Excuse me. Chihuahua. I'on know who you thought you was bringing your lil short ass in here but—"

Her hand lifted, and the only reason Gotti stopped

talking was because he was so surprised by the disrespect. She *clearly* had no idea who he was. Taking a deep breath, Gotti began to pace and pray.

"Uh, Rue," Raul said quietly. "I appreciate you taking up for me, but you really need to calm down."

"Calm down?" She scoffed. "This man walks in here firing you with no explanation as to why, and you're telling me to calm down?"

"I'll find out the reasons when I get my termination letter. That doesn't matter to me right now. Right now, all that matters to me is our safety." He tried to grab her arm, but she jerked it away. "We need to go."

"No! Are you crazy? What the hell is wrong with you?"

The office phone rang, and Rue quickly picked it up and put it on speakerphone. "Yes?"

"Ms. Williams, I have Mr. Gambino Nahtahn on line one."

"Oh shit," Raul grumbled, taking backwards steps.

"Put him through," Rue advised.

A few seconds passed before Gotti heard his voice clearly through the speaker. "Who am I speaking with?"

"Rue Williams."

"Rue, is my brother Gotti in the office with you?"

"If he's the one you sent to fire Raul, yes."

"Is Raul still there?"

"Yes."

"Unharmed?"

Rue hesitated, brows wrinkling. "Uh, yes."

"Is my brother quiet? Calm? Pacing, perhaps?"

"All three."

Gambino chuckled. "Okay, Ms. Williams. I need you to get Raul out of the office immediately. I will not be able to stop my brother from severely hurting or even killing that man. As of this morning, Raul's employment has been terminated. Gotti Nahtahn is his replacement. Whatever he says goes."

Not bothering to wait for her to respond, Gambino disconnected the call.

Rue huffed and was about to complain, but Raul grabbed his phone off the desk and ran, not even bothering to get his briefcase. Had Rue not been so confused by what was going on, she would have found it amusing.

Gotti lifted his cell phone to his ear and answered the call. Only a few seconds passed before he said, "Big brotha, you gon' have to find somebody else to do this. It wasn't even him. It's this lil short ass—aight but if she—but you don't even know wh—aight bet." Gotti growled as his eyes shifted toward Rue and sized her up. "I'll be on my best behavior." His head shook as he squeezed the bridge of his nose. His eyes rolled to the ceiling as he released a long exhale. With a very monotone voice he said, "I promise not to hit anyone today. Love."

After ending the call, Gotti connected his eyes with Rue's. She may not have realized it, but Gambino had just saved both her *and* Raul's life. Gotti hadn't been in the building for a full thirty minutes yet, and he was already ready to say fuck that shit. The only thing that made him continue with the agreement was his mother's legacy and not wanting to fail.

"You can go back to your cubicle," he said, wanting to get under her skin.

Her chin jutted and shoulders straightened. "I don't have a cubicle. My office is next door actually. I'm the head of the design department and a supervisor."

"Good for you. Now get out."

Her eyes squinted, and Gotti couldn't hold his smile in.

She had the prettiest pecan brown skin he'd ever seen. Her eyes were slanted, and she had pretty bowtie shaped lips. Tight curls framed her diamond shaped face. She looked magical. Like a fairy. A fiery, feisty fairy. Gotti wanted to bend her over the desk and fuck some of that fire out of her.

"Raul might be scared of you, but I'm not."

"You're also not smart, because if you knew who I was..." Gotti closed the space between them. His tone lowered when he added, "You would be." With his eyes lifted toward the open door, he told her, "If you want to have a civilized conversation with me about why Raul was fired, we can do that later. For now, I will not tell you to leave again. If you're not out of here in three seconds, I will remove you myself."

A frown covered her face as she looked him from head to toe. "As if I'd let you touch me."

She walked away, and Gotti's smile returned. His eyes lowered to her ass. It was small like her but round and poking out.

Maybe he'd have fun there after all.

19

R^{ue}

As Rue devoured her French bread dipped in herbed oil, she looked over all the information her best friend, Ashley, sent her about the Nahtahn family. In all her years of working at *Nahtahn Designs*, she never had the slightest clue they were a mafia family. Granted, that wasn't the kind of thing one loudly talked about unless they were looking for attention, but still. There were no whispered conversations or gossip to suggest Claire had been the wife of the don. But apparently, mostly everyone in the office knew—except Rue.

"Maybe it's because you're technically from Memphis," Ashley said, "but either way, they aren't to be fucked with. Especially Gotti. He's the youngest brother and the one that's always in pussy or trouble. If he's your new boss, you definitely need to be on your good girl shit. They don't tolerate disrespect from anyone. I'm surprised he even let you talk to him the way you did."

Rue rolled her eyes as she dipped another piece of bread into the oil. "Please. All those men are alike. Gotti won't touch me. I'd even go as far as to say I turned him on. He's probably used to people cowering in front of him, but I will never do that."

"Look, all I'm going to say is be careful. You're so sweet and kind, Rue. Show him that side of you. Please don't think what happened today will happen tomorrow. I don't want anything to happen to you."

The fear and tremble in Ashley's voice alarmed Rue. Putting her stubborn armor aside, Rue considered her best friend's words. Though she'd dated a few bad boys and drug dealers before, none of them were of the Nahtahn caliber. Maybe she did need to tread lightly.

"I hear you."

"I'm not saying you have to apologize, but at least make it clear to him you want peace the next time you talk. Not just for your physical safety but the safety of your job too. Until you know what led to Raul being fired, you might want to be careful, Rue."

Rue sighed as she nodded and squeezed the back of her neck. "You're right. I won't go against my principles to kiss his ass, but I'll be kind and professional."

"Good. That's my girl. Now... Is he as fine up close as he appears from a distance? I've never seen any of them brothers up close but, chile, they all look so sexy."

Now that Rue wasn't brewing with anger, she could allow herself to admit Gotti was attractive. In fact, he was one of the most attractive men she'd ever seen. He was tall and slim but muscular. His physique was covered in caramel brown skin that had a golden undertone.

Tight eyes grew tighter and looked almost closed when he was upset. Thick, straight brows hovered over them. He had juicy blunt brown lips encased by a thick beard that Rue admittedly wanted to moisturize with her cum. Clearing her throat, she ran her hand down her neck and squeezed her thighs together. The *last* thing she needed was to be attracted to Gotti Nahtahn.

Though he was the brother closest to her age at twenty-six, he was also the one who headlined news articles because of his wild and reckless behavior the most.

"I mean... he's fine. But his attitude makes him ugly. Okay, I can't even lie like that. Gotti is fine as hell."

They shared a cackle before gossiping a little while longer. After ending the call, Rue showered and climbed into bed to watch a home improvement show and relax. She truly loved art and design of all kinds, but interior design had become her favorite. Rue loved turning nothing, literally an empty space, into something beautiful. Something so many people called home. That was what she and Claire had in common. Just at the thought of Claire's son she groaned... unsure of how things would play out at the office tomorrow.

The Next Morning

RUE SLIPPED INTO GOTTI'S OFFICE WITH HASTE, wanting to leave what she had before she lost her nerve. She set the donut holes and coffee on the desk. After snatching a Post-it note, she scribbled a quick note.

Don't be an asshole or read too much into this. It's not an apology because I wasn't wrong. It is, however, a sweet treat and hope for a sweeter start. P.S. Don't make me regret this—Rue

Pleased with her note, she set it in front of the coffee and donut holes and went back to her office. It felt like forever passed with her waiting for Gotti to arrive. He'd have to walk by her office to get to his, and every time someone walked by, her eyes shot up to see if it was him.

When he finally did arrive an hour later, her heart dropped, and a part of her wanted to scramble to get what she'd left on his desk before he saw it. Pulling in a deep breath, she calmed herself and assured herself that she'd done the right thing.

Only a few minutes passed before Gotti was lightly tapping on her door. He looked good in his black on black suit and shirt. Clearing her throat of its nerves, she told him he could come in.

"Thank you," he muttered, holding the donuts.

"You're welcome," she grumbled, making him smile.

"Would you... like one?"

Instead of immediately saying no, she considered that was his way of extending the olive branch back to her.

"I didn't take you as the type to share," she teased, unable to stop herself.

"I'm not, so you should feel special."

Her smile spread against her wishes as he walked over to her desk and extended the donuts in her direction.

"Thank you, Mr. Nahtahn."

"Gotti," he corrected, before walking away.

20

Gotti

CLAIRE SAT NEXT TO GOTTI AND TOOK HIS HAND INTO
hers. Instantly, calm consumed him. His brother's teased him
for being a mama's boy, but with Claire Nahtahn, that was
the only place he felt true peace. While others were able to go
to spouses, hobbies, or even God, none of those things worked
for Gotti the way his mother's presence did.

"Why are you out here hiding when there's a party going
on?" Claire asked.

"No reason."

"Lie again."

Gotti chuckled. "You swear you know me."

"I do. I gave birth to you. I know you better than you
know yourself." Claire cupped his cheek and turned his face
toward her. "Talk to Mommy, and tell me what's wrong."

Briefly, Gotti considered how honest he wanted to be

with her. Though he trusted her, there were some seeds that
were better left buried. If he confided in his mother, he knew
what he said would stay between them, but he didn't want to
risk her feeling a pressure to guard what he told her if it went
against what was best for the family.

"I fucked up."

"Then let's fix it. What happened?"

Gotti's head tilted as he sighed. "This girl I was messing
with... she was a plant. I thought it was just about sex, but
she was sent to get close to me."

Claire's spine straightened and head tilted. "Close to you
for what? What did she do or take?"

"It was a setup. She tried to drug me so the niggas could
come in and do whatever. Luckily, I didn't just drink the
drink. I started testing my drinks after what happened to
Mira at the club three years ago," Gotti informed, referring to
one of his cousin's that was drugged and then held for
ransom by one of their enemies.

"So what happened?"

"I switched the drinks, and she passed out. Like thirty
minutes later, four dudes came bursting through the door. I
had to lay them all down."

"When was this?" Claire asked, squeezing his shoulder.
"And why didn't you tell your brothers?"

"It happened last night, and I didn't tell them because I
handled it myself. I didn't want to hear their mouths. They
already feel like I deal with too many women." Gotti sucked
his teeth and ran his hands down his face. "All I keep
thinking about is what would have happened if I would have
had that drink. I'd probably be dead right now. All because I
wanted some pus—some companionship."

Claire chuckled. "First, I'm glad you're alive and well
and here with me. Second, I think that was meant to be a

wakeup call for you. Your brothers and Cory can tell you to slow down, but you won't make that change until you're ready." Gotti nodded his agreement. *"I know you might think you're just having fun, but you're Gotti Nahtahn. The last thing we need is for your fun to lead to failure. Or death. Or hell, disease or a baby that will tie you to the wrong woman and family. Gambino was right when he told you that your life would change if you started operating out of a place of self-respect and discipline. I want you to start having more power and self-control. And if this is some kind of addiction that you need professional help for..."*

Gotti's head shook. *"Nah, it ain't that deep. I love sex but I can stop whenever I want to. After what happened last night, I'ma get it together. I know women have been a weakness for a lot of powerful men in the past and I don't want that to be the case with me. I'ma get it together."*

"Good. Now, come on in here and cheer up. You did well last night. You relied on your gut and kept yourself safe. I'm proud of you, Son."

Gotti flicked a tear away at the memory of his mother. Life hadn't been the same without her. He'd felt lonelier and like his best source of peace had been taken away. Though he'd tried to find other ways to give himself peace and happiness, nothing he did could compare with the bond he shared with his mother.

He looked over the plan for the scholarships he wanted to give out in Claire's name. Now that he was temporarily the CEO of her company, he wanted to do something positive in her name and give him something constructive to focus on. For the last six months, he'd been staying as active as he could to stay out of trouble. Six scholarships would be given out a year. The scholarship would cover housing in Rose Valley Hills through Chapel and Jeremy or through

Armor and Remedy in Jasper Lane. It would also include interior decorating from the company for every area in the homes.

If Gotti had it his way, people would be impacted by his mother for years to come. After sending the plan to Kayla for her to look over before he took the idea to his brothers, Gotti headed out of the office for the day. He couldn't help but pause briefly and look into Rue's office through the small window on her door. Her chair was turned to the side as she smiled at whatever whoever she was talking to on the phone said.

From what Gotti could see, she had a beautiful smile, and he wished it was directed toward him. Though they may have gotten off on the wrong foot, he appreciated her gesture that morning. Gotti wasn't sure if it would change anything between them, but it showed him that she was willing to compromise. He could also tell that she was stubborn and probably hated making the first move, so he'd do something to meet her halfway. But he couldn't deny how entertaining and amusing it was to get under her beautiful skin.

By the time Gotti had made it home, he'd received a text from Kayla telling him to call her. She was the only woman outside of his mother that Gotti trusted and felt safe with, and he was truly glad she and Gambino had worked things out. They wanted to get married last fall, but between business picking up and Gambino gifting Kayla a building for her bookstore, they slowed down and agreed to take their time so the wedding would be all she wanted it to be.

Once he'd showered and changed into something more comfortable, Gotti called her.

"Hey, bro," Kayla answered, and hearing the smile in her tone made Gotti smile.

"Wassup, sis? What you think?"

"I think that's an amazing idea, and a wonderful use for your money. Mama would be so proud of you, and I am too."

Gotti blushed as he ran his hand down his chest. "I appreciate that. Thank you. This means a lot to me. I just wanted to do some for her myself, you know?"

"I hear you. I'm so excited! I know this is your passion project to honor her, but let me know if you need help with absolutely anything, okay?"

"I will, sis. I'll see you in a few. I'm about to have Lu meet me over there so I can tell him and Bino about it."

"Yay! See you soon."

A genuine smile spread Gotti's lips as he texted his brothers in their group chat. With Kayla's encouragement, he was finally confident enough to tell his brothers about his idea.

21

R^{ue} The Next Monday

RUE HUMMED AS SHE LEFT THE CONFERENCE ROOM. She'd just finished a meeting with a potential client and was pleased with how the meeting went. Normally, she didn't bring in new clients and only talked to them when it was time for her to start coming up with mockups for their home. Since Raul was gone, the order in which things were done had changed. Rue wasn't sure how long it would last, but for now, she was more hands on with the whole process from start to finish.

Everyone had been on edge since Gotti arrived for more reasons than one. Not only were they afraid he'd fire them too, but his presence provided a sense of danger that kept them all on their toes. For a brief moment, Rue wondered how that felt. To be so feared people hesitated to talk to you. Get close to you. For a brief moment, she wondered if he had anyone who chose to be in his life, not just family and workers who were required. Then, she reminded herself of how he talked to and treated Raul his first day there, and that convinced her to care less.

She convinced herself that he was a bully and that he didn't deserve her thoughts. But every time their eyes locked around the office, that was easier to say than actually feel.

When she stepped into her office and saw several bouquets of roses on her desk, she dropped the file she was holding as she gasped. Twelve different colored bouquets of roses awaited her, and she had no idea who they were from.

"I didn't know what color you'd prefer, so I got a few."

At the sound of Gotti's voice behind her, Rue jumped and turned to face him.

"Huh?"

His head nodded in the direction of the roses. "The flowers. I didn't know which one to get you."

"Oh." Releasing a nervous chuckle, Rue looked back at the flowers as her eyes watered. "You didn't have to get me any, but yellow is my favorite color."

"Good. I'll keep that in mind."

When she turned to face him, she jumped, because he was closer than she expected. The gesture had completely caught her by surprise, and she didn't know what the hell to do with herself.

"Um... they're beautiful. Thank you. But... why?"

Licking his lips, Gotti pulled his hands behind his back. "We didn't have a good introduction to one another. I want to take you to dinner to rectify that."

Her mouth opened and closed, but she was in such disbelief she couldn't respond. Rue ran her hand up and down her leg.

"I appreciate it, but that's not necessary. I think we're good."

Gotti's chuckle was barely audible as his head tilted while he rubbed his palms together. "So good you avoid me, barely look at me, and send messages to me through everyone else so we don't have to talk?" Rue was unable to deny that, so she remained silent. "I suggested dinner so we could get to know each other a little. Hopefully if you spent a little time with me, you wouldn't think I was a..." Gotti tapped his chin and looked toward the ceiling as if he was in deep thought. "Bully."

Rue gasped before she groaned and covered her face in shame. When she said that in the breakroom the first day he arrived, she wasn't expecting it to get back to him.

"I don't honestly care about what you think about me," Gotti continued, "but you're one of three supervisors I will be working closely with while I'm here. And seeing as I need to name someone my replacement when my time here is over, I'd think you would want to make sure you and I are good so things will remain fair."

"I want my work and contributions around here to speak for themselves, but you're right, we do need to get over that so we can work together." She paused and nodded, needing to build herself up to say, "Okay. We can do dinner."

His eyes slowly grazed her frame before a small smirk lifted the corner of his mouth. "I'll stop by your office after work tomorrow and we can head out."

"Okay," she agreed softly, and she didn't realize she was holding her breath until he walked away.

22

G otti

Dinner hadn't quite gone as Gotti would have expected. They ate in silence and didn't talk at all. When it was time for dessert, he decided to at least let Rue in on why Raul had been fired and hoped that would cause her to relax a bit. So she wouldn't just have to take his word for it, he slid a folder over that had screenshots of Raul's email correspondence and a spreadsheet of the amount of clients they'd lost and retained over the past year.

"As you can see," Gotti started, "Raul was very disrespectful while talking to quite a few clients. On top of that, we lost six clients since he was in charge and didn't bring in more than two new ones. A lot of potential clients were lost because he didn't follow up on setting up meetings. And if they did meet with representatives, Raul didn't finalize the onboarding process, and they went to our competition."

A frown covered her beautiful face as she flipped from one page to the next. With disgust, she shoved the folder into the middle of the table.

"Well, I see why he was fired. I did overreact, but that's only because I didn't know what was going on. I apologize for that."

"Don't apologize for protecting someone you thought was being done wrong."

She smiled softly but twisted her mouth to the side to hide it.

"Seeing that changed everything. Whatever you need my help with to get our numbers up, I'll do. Customer service was big to your mom, and she'd hate it if she knew anyone spoke to our clients like."

His head bobbed once. He hated when people spoke about his mother in past tense, because it was a reminder that she was gone. He suffered dealing with that enough.

"From what I hear, you have a great personality and clients love you."

She giggled. "I guess you find that hard to believe huh?"

"I mean seeing as you was biting at my ankles the day we met yeah." They shared a laugh before he continued. "But if you could handle meeting with potential clients for me that would be great. I know that's technically not your job, but I think they would receive you better than me."

"I agree, and I can do that."

Silence found them for a while. Their waitress came to retrieve payment for the bill and a hefty tip. When she left, Gotti said, "I know dinner is over, but I still feel like I don't know you. Ask me anything you want to make you feel comfortable enough to tell me something about you."

Only a beat of silence passed before she asked, "Are you lonely?"

His head jerked and brows wrinkled at the sound of her question. Not answering right away, Gotti held her gaze. She stood and shrugged her blazer off her shoulders. When she turned to put it on the back of her chair, his eyes lowered to her ass in the slinky slip dress she had on. Gotti loved that style on a woman because it accentuated her curves. As small as Rue was, Gotti would never deny her feminine shape. Licking his lips, he adjusted himself in his seat as his dick hardened.

"Gotti?" she called as she sat back down. "I asked are you lonely?"

"Why you ask that?"

She shrugged and briefly avoided his eyes. "Just something I wondered about earlier. The way people act around you at the office had me curious."

"How they act?"

"In awe of you or afraid of you. No in between. It made me wonder if you had any real friends in your life. People who choose to love you outside of your family. Do you have real friends?" Her smile was soft as she grabbed her glass of water. "Maybe I let the books and movies get to me and you're not this big, bad monster that people find unapproachable. Between that and how we first met—"

"Yeah, I get it." He stroked his beard as he considered her question. No one had ever asked him such an intimate question, and Gotti honestly didn't know how to respond. It was his natural instinct to lie to protect himself and not let anyone in. However, a part of him wondered if this was a chance to connect with a woman in a way he never had before. "I do have friends. My brothers and cousins are also some of my best friends, but I do have three friends that I'm not related to. One is my future sister-in-law. The other two I met in college. I could consider them close friends, but their careers and families sent them to different states."

"You went to college?"

"Yeah." The surprise on her face made him chuckle. "I might talk country and with slang at times but I ain't no dumb nigga, Rue."

"Oh, no. Yeah, I didn't think that. I mean, you code switch well. I didn't think you were dumb. I'm just surprised to hear you actually went to college. The way people talk about you—"

"I invited you here so you could get to know me for yourself." She nodded with a smile and urged him to continue. "So yeah, I have three close friends outside of family, but I get why you would think it would be hard for someone like me to maintain genuine friendships. It's hard to trust and let people in. I don't actively seek new friends at all. Even if they were genuine, they wouldn't understand my lifestyle. That's why me and my brothers and cousins are so close." He paused. "To answer your question... yeah. Sometimes I am lonely. Especially now that my ma is gone. The only other woman I'm close to is my sister, so maybe I am more lonely for the companionship of a woman. Not a mother because no one can replace her, but the softness and femininity of the opposite sex."

"Hmm... I didn't think you'd be the type to have trouble with female companionship."

"Pussy is one thing. That's *very* easy to get. I'm referring to something deeper."

"And that's something you actually want?"

"I haven't. I didn't think I did until I just said that shit."

"Glad I could help." Her smile was genuine as she stared into his eyes.

"You wanna help me with that?"

"Being lonely?" The innocence in her tone made his heart skip a beat.

"Yeah."

"What did you have in mind?"

Gotti extended his arm across the table. When she put her hand inside of his, he helped her stand and walk around the table. After sitting her on his lap, she moaned quickly at the feel of his dick as he wrapped his arm around her waist.

"This is breaking all kinds of HR rules," she said with a chuckle.

"Good thing I'm the boss... and I don't give a fuck."

His lips went to her neck, and she gripped his arm.

"I... I don't want to just fuck you, Gotti."

He pulled away and looked into her eyes. "But you *do* want to fuck me?" Instead of answering him vocally, Rue slipped his hand under her dress. "Ooh," escaped him at the feel of her warm wetness.

"Does that answer your question?"

"Hell yeah. So what else do you want?" he asked, pushing her panties to the side and sliding his middle finger into her soaking wet pussy.

"I want to know you," she confessed breathlessly. "That's what just turned me on. I... mm..." Her arm wrapped around his neck tightly as his finger turned upward and curved. "I want to be your favorite person."

His movement inside of her stopped. "Why?"

"Because just a week ago you were my *least* favorite person."

When hearty laughter erupted from the pit of Gotti's belly, he had no choice but to remove his finger from her pussy. And her serious expression only made it funnier.

"Yo' ass a trip. I'ma call you my lil chihuahua."

"Oh God no. Call me Rue or come up with something better than that."

"But chihuahuas are cute. You feisty and mean but I like that shit."

"Mhm." Her smile returned as she looked at his lips. Rue didn't kiss them like he thought she would, and Gotti was cool with that, because kissing wasn't really his thing. She did, however, run her thumb over his lips. "I'm not mean. I'm actually really nice. I just don't play about the people I care about."

"Well, if you wanna be my favorite person, you need to put me at the top of the list of people you care about," Gotti requested, surprising himself. Before she could agree, he pinched her cheek and made her laugh as he added, "You're the most beautiful woman I've ever seen."

Her bottom lip poked out, and she rested her forehead against his. "I feel like this is moving really fast."

"Do you want it to stop?"

Her head shook as she confessed, "No. I want you to kiss me."

And he did. Deeply. Tenderly. Passionately. When he pulled away he told her, "I ain't tryna pressure you but if you ain't tryna fuck, you need to go to your side of the table."

She smiled as she wiped her lipstick off his mouth. "You don't have self-control?"

That was the first time he'd been asked that and struggled to say yes. "Yeah, but I ain't tryna have it right now with you."

Up until that point, everything Gotti did, he did by choice. It was intentional. But when it came down to Rue

Williams, what he said and how he felt seemed to be beyond his control.

Rue stood, leading him to believe she was about to move. She made him like her a little more when she said, "Are you coming, or not?"

23

R ue

GOTTI'S HANDS WERE ALL OVER HER WHEN THEY stumbled into their suite at *The Rose Valley Hotel*. It had been so long since a man touched her in a way that wasn't cordial or threatening, and she wanted to savor every second. Her body shuddered when he picked her up and tossed her onto the bed. She wanted to tell him that it had been a while and to take his time with her, but between him being a mafia capo and the urgency in which he undressed, she could tell slow and steady wasn't his style.

Her eyes froze on his dick. In true tall, slim man fashion, Gotti had the longest dick she'd ever seen. It was meaty and veiny just like she liked. Rue wasn't sure if she'd be able to fit all of him inside her pussy and throat, but she was damn sure going to try.

After grabbing a condom from his wallet, Gotti climbed into bed with her.

"Have you changed your mind yet?" he checked, to which she shook her head. "No, chihuahua. I need to hear you say that shit."

Rue chuckled as much as she didn't want to. "Gotti, do *not* call me that. I'm serious," she warned, snapping her legs shut.

"Aight, aight. Is bae okay? Does that work?"

For some reason, the softened tone he used made her heart skip a beat. Bashfully, she nodded. "Bae works."

"Good," he mumbled against her lips before kissing them. His hand lowered to her bottom set of lips. Not long passed before two fingers were inside of her and he was hitting her spot.

When her ridges began to swell against him, she pulled away and moaned. "Oh wow. You found that really, really quick."

His laugh was arrogant as he curved his fingers upward. "That's usually what happens when you know what you doing."

"Oh fuck," she whimpered as her wetness increased, growing so loudly it warned him that she was about to squirt before she could. He continued to massage her spot until the squirting liquid ceased, then he pulled his fingers out.

"Turn around," he demanded while using her leg to turn her around. The forceful way in which he manhandled her turned her on. Gotti arched her back and told her, "Stay just like that. Don't you fucking move."

She crossed her ankles as her pussy throbbed in anticipation. Everything about him and their exchange was heightening her arousal. Once he had the condom on, Gotti made his way behind her. As soon as he spread her cheeks and began to press his way inside of her, she moaned.

"Shit," he groaned. "This pussy tight as fuck. You gon' let me in?"

"Mhm," she moaned, wanting it all.

Rue cried out as he stretched her.

When she thought she couldn't take anymore, she yelped and pushed him out of her. Gotti chuckled as he pulled her back and held her hands against her back.

"Relax, bae. You fuckin' a nigga wit' a big dick. That's all."

"That's all?" she replied animatedly as he pushed his way back in, making Gotti laugh.

"Yeah, relax." He went slower that time, pulling out and covering himself with more of her nectar before pushing in deeper. "That's it. Open up that pussy."

"Mmm..."

"That's it."

Once he was finally all the way in, Gotti pulled out. His first few strokes were slow, but the moment he sensed she was comfortable enough to fuck him back, he picked up the pace. Quiet gasps for air escaped her as he grunted. Her body weakened and toes curled as her spine tingled.

He was so deep, all she could feel was him. Rue couldn't believe her body was reacting to him the way it was and that she was about to cum already. After she did, he deepened her arch and pulled out, only stroking her spot.

"Oh fuck. Oh shit," she moaned, gripping the bed and trying to scoot up. The sensation building was overwhelming.

"Stop running and take this dick."

"Ah!" she yelped when he smacked her ass, but it quickly turned into a moan. "Gotti," she whimpered.

"Hmm?" Her mouth hung open. She could barely breathe let alone speak. All she could do was whine as she came. "Yesss, bae. Give me all that gushy shit."

Rue's eyes squeezed shut as she trembled against him, causing Gotti to lay her flat on her back. His strokes slowed to a medium, hard pace as he hit a spot that was like a detonator, causing her to squirt and cry out. No man had ever handled her body the way Gotti was, and she was so overwhelmed Rue didn't know how she felt about it.

Before Sunrise

RUE SNUCK OUT OF THE SUITE AND ORDERED A TOWN car before Gotti woke up. She *desperately* needed to get her mind together before she faced him at work. Last night, he made her cum ten times before he tapped out. No man had *ever* done anything near that. As orgasmic and pleasurable as the experience was, something was missing. While she enjoyed it, it felt like they were disconnected. Maybe it was because they'd just met but having such a climactic physical exchange with a man had her feeling more vulnerable than she ever had before.

As she hopped out of the town car, she texted Ashley to see if she was awake yet so they could talk. She was so consumed by her thoughts that she wasn't paying attention to her surroundings or the fact that her ex Alex was waiting for her.

"Where the fuck you been?"

At the sound of his voice, she shrieked and jumped. Clutching her chest, she tried to remain casual as she looked at the man she once loved. That love faded every time he lied, cheated, put his gang before her, or abused her. Alex would always downplay the abuse because he never hit her with a closed fist. He would say the choking, pushing, and slapping were just anger when they argued. That worked about three times before Rue remembered abuse of any kind was never love.

"A-Alex... What are you doing here?"

"I asked you a question." Alex pushed himself off the gate and stepped toward her. Feeling her body shrink to make room for him took Rue to a place she hated having to go back to. Though they'd broken up, Alex made it clear she was his every time he saw her. This was the first time he'd ever been at her apartment. She'd taken special care to make sure he didn't know where she stayed when she moved out.

"How did you know where I live?"

"That don't matter. Who you been fucking that you just now getting home?"

"Alex, I—"

"Did you think I was playing when I told you you were mine?"

When he gripped her neck and pulled her into him, she knew better than to swing. Instead, she pressed her balled fists into his chest to push him away. Because unlike her first rowdy encounter with Gotti, there was no doubt in her mind that things with Alex would get violent.

"Alex, please..."

"Are you alright, Rue?"

Relief filled her at the sound of the doorman's voice. Alex released her instantly. "I'm fine," she assured him, taking fast steps in his direction. Once they were inside and he had the door closed, she told him, "Please take a picture of him for security and make sure he's *never* let in."

"Yes, ma'am."

Rue's heart raced as she headed toward the elevators. Though no one could make it to her floor unless they were on her approved list, people could still wander around the building and lower levels. The last thing she needed was for Alex to get inside and wait for her to come out.

"Fuck," she gritted, trying to fight back her tears as she scanned her key card to get to her floor. It was one thing for her to dismiss Alex when they were out in public together. Now that he knew where she lived, there was no telling *what* he would do.

Lunchtime

RUE NIBBLED HER LIP AS SHE WAITED FOR ASHLEY TO answer. She'd called her earlier, but Rue was on a call. Thankfully, Gotti hadn't come in yet, but she didn't know how long that would last. Between thinking about their night together and running into Alex, Rue had been struggling to focus all day. She was considering leaving early after she finished a mockup for one of her newer clients.

"Hey, best friend," Ashley answered, and Rue smiled. Though she was close to her parents and sister, they all still lived in Memphis. She'd met Ashley when she moved to Rose Valley Hills for college, and they'd been inseparable ever since.

"Poooh, I needed you this morning. Shit's only gotten worse."

"Oh no! What happened?"

"No judgment, but after dinner with Gotti yesterday, we spent the night at a hotel."

Ashley released a bark of laughter. "Wait what? How

did you go from hating him to having sex with him?" After telling Ashley about the flowers and their dinner conversation, Ashley followed up with, "So how was it? *Please* tell me he had a big dick. He's too fine not to have a big dick."

Rue sniggled as she sat back in her seat. "I'll just say that saying about skinny niggas having big dicks rang to be very true for Gotti. And he knew how to use it. The man made me cum like ten times, sis. No exaggeration."

"Oookay? So what's the reason for the distress in your tone?"

With a sigh, Rue stood and looked out of the window out into the city. "Physically, Gotti was the best man I've ever been with. But if I wanted to just cum with no emotional or mental connection, I could have gone home and used my vibrator. And I know we don't know each other well, so I wasn't expecting him to make love to me. I don't know. It just felt like it was literally just about cumming. And he made me cum a lot. I feel crazy even saying this."

"No, I get it. When you are physically intimate with someone, you want mental and emotional intimacy too. That's a biblical definition of sex. Yada—to know. So you're not wrong. Not everyone can have sex with no strings attached, no feelings. You're one of them ones."

Rue smiled. That was exactly why she'd been wanting to talk to her best friend. She knew Ashley would help her make sense of her muddled thoughts.

"So are you going to let it be just a onetime thing?" Ashley asked.

"Now that I'm not sure about. I feel like this is just how he is, and I get it. I'm sure he has sex with a lot of women, so he doesn't care about anything other than the release. But I want more. I don't want to feel like I'm trying to change him, you know?"

"I feel you. Well, I guess you can just wait and see what he's on. If he wants to have sex again, just be honest with him. If he isn't willing to give you more intimacy, then don't sleep with him."

"Yeah, maybe that's what I'll do. We will be working together for a while, so I don't want to make things weird between us. I do really like him, and it happened fast. I don't even know why I like him. It's just something that I'm drawn to."

"I hope it works in your favor. Just be careful. Gotti isn't the average man. You just got away from Alex's crazy ass. I don't want you mixed up with another man who doesn't mean you well."

At that point, Rue didn't even want to tell Ashley about her encounter with Alex. She changed the subject, and they continued to talk until her lunch was delivered. When she was done eating, she spent the next two hours working on the mockup for her client before leaving early.

24

G otti

The Next Day

GOTTI WAS IMPRESSED WITH THE PROGRESS HE AND the supervisors had made so far. In just under two weeks, they'd retained several new clients, fixed relationships with current clients, and came up with plans to secure future clients. He didn't care as much about the employees needs and concerns until he thought about what Rue said while they were at dinner. It made him think about the strained interactions he'd been having while there. Initially, he didn't care as long as no one disrespected him. Then, he considered how Claire ran the business as if they were all family and wanted to change that.

When an idea came to mind, he called Gambino and hoped he answered. Gotti was becoming more and more invested in the interior design company, which was surprising to him. It wasn't the design itself, because he had no interest in that. It was more about fixing something that was broken. Gotti took great pleasure in being able to do that. Doing it for his mother's business made it mean that much more.

"You good, baby boy?"

"I'm great actually. I wanted to give you an update and run an idea by you."

"Aw yeah? Wassup?"

"Aight, so I was thinking we could have a lil company party. I think my presence has a lot of people on edge. They walk around on eggshells, and I want them comfortable here. Now I ain't saying I'ma be involved, but I think it'll be a good look if I paid someone to get a party together so they could relax afterhours and enjoy themselves."

"I think that's a good idea. Company parties often lead to closeness with employees too. Definitely set that up. I'll grab Lu and me and my kitten will come through too."

"Aight, bet. Also, I've brought in five new clients so far. I'm working on bringing two back. One is the real estate developer that wanted us to design all of her staging for her properties, so I definitely want her back. And the other was for the commercial developer that was looking for one of the decorators to design his new high rise a couple of blocks down. I'on too much care about the residential clients we've lost. Those are easy to replace."

"I feel you, and you're right. If we can avoid losing those two, that would be good. That's millions in profit a year from just those two alone."

"Right. It's taking a few talks, but I think it's working. More than anything, they want to make sure we're stable and dedicated to working with them. And for what they would be paying, I can respect that."

Gambino didn't respond right away, causing Gotti to

pull the phone from his ear to make sure the call was still connected.

"Aye, I'm really proud of you, baby brotha. I knew you had it in you, but seeing it in real time is different. Just know Ma and Pops looking down on you proud. I hope you're proud of yourself too."

A sense of accomplishment filled Gotti at his brother's words. "That means a lot to me, big brotha. For real. I know I used to be on a lot of rah-rah shit, but I can't lie and say focusing on business isn't helping and making me feel good. I still wanna get back in the streets and fuck some shit up, but I'on mind staying hands on with the legal businesses when they need me."

"That's what I wanna hear. I meant to tell you, though, get with that Rue Williams girl. She's a supervisor, but she's also head of design. Before that, she was the client care manager, so I'm sure she can help bring in even more clients."

Gotti chuckled and tugged his bottom lip between his teeth. "I've gotten with Rue already," he said, dick hardening just thinking about their night together. He didn't want to tell his brother that he'd gotten inside her too, because he didn't want to hear Gambino's mouth. Rue wasn't just a fuck to him. He actually cared about her and wanted to spend time with her. She was the first woman he wanted to get to know and see if he could have a future with.

"Cool. Well, Lu and I—"

"Aye, Bino, I'ma stop by your house when I get off," Gotti said as he saw Rue briskly make her way down the hall and pass his office.

"Aight, coo—"

Quickly disconnecting the call, Gotti stood and went

after her. Her steps picked up into a light jog before she rushed into the restroom. Clearly something was wrong with her. Not bothering to wait, he went into the multi-stall bathroom. Ignoring the women gasping at his presence, he yelled, "Rue," as he walked between the stalls.

"Gotti?" she called quietly. "What the hell are you doing in here?"

"Are you okay? You looked upset."

She sniffled. "Can we talk about this in my office? You're not supposed to be in here."

Gotti sucked his teeth. "I'on give a fuck about allat."

"I'll be right out, Gotti. I promise."

"Aight," he agreed unwillingly before leaving and going to her office.

Only a minute or so passed before she timidly stepped inside. Her eyes were red and her nose was too. It was clear she'd been crying. Instinctively, Gotti pulled her into his arms.

"What's wrong, chih—bae?"

She giggled. "I hate that name, but I needed that laugh," she admitted, holding him tightly. "My childhood dog died this morning. He was sixteen so it was kind of expected but still. I had him since I was ten and just knew he had at least four more years. The only reason I didn't bring him here with me from Memphis was because of school and crazy work hours. Now I hate I only went to see him two weekends out of the month."

Gotti felt the pull to be soft with her. To be affectionate. That was something he never did. It felt foreign cupping her cheeks and looking into her eyes, but it was what he was led to do.

After gracing her with a sweet kiss he said, "I'm sorry for your loss, Rue. What kind of dog was it?"

Her nostrils flared and she clenched her jaw. "I don't want to say," she whined.

"Why not?"

"His name was Chalupa. He was a... chihuahua."

He stared at her for a few seconds before bursting into laughter. When her tiny fist punched his stomach, Gotti laughed harder.

"I *know* you fucking lying. That's why your ass act the way you do. Let me see him."

"No! Stop laughing at Lupa."

"Lupa?" he repeated through his laughter. When she groaned and tried to leave the office, Gotti grabbed her and pulled her into his arms as he tried to stop laughing. "I'm sorry, bae. Do you need the rest of the day off?"

"No, I'll just cry looking at pictures and videos of him. We're going to have a funeral for him Saturday."

"Can I come? I want to be there for you."

Her eyes rolled as he kissed her neck, but she smiled. "Not if you're going to crack jokes."

"Only if it'll make you smile. I do want to be there for you, though."

"That would be nice," she muttered, turning in his arms. "I'll show you Chalupa, but you better not laugh."

"I can't make any promises, bae."

With a smile, she walked over to her desk and grabbed her phone. After going to her photos, she handed the phone to him. Gotti covered his mouth as he stared at the picture.

"They say pet owners can look like their dogs sometimes. Y'all got the same spirit, small head, *and* pointy nose. If you were a shade lighter, y'all would be twins."

"Gotti!" she yelled.

"Aight, I'm done!"

After Work

GOTTI WASN'T USED TO CATERING TO A WOMAN, BUT for Rue, he wanted to try. She didn't have an appetite, but he grabbed her some soup on the way to his home anyway. The fact that he took her to Nahtahn Cove instead of her place said a lot. She was the first woman he'd ever brought home.

After she finished her soup, he let her shower and change into one of his shirts, which looked like a dress on her. They watched HGTV but he was bored of it, so he started to massage her body. As she lay flat on her stomach, he couldn't resist sliding his fingers between her legs to play with her pussy. Before he could relish in the suction of her walls, she pushed his hand away and scooted up the bed. Rue sat up and pulled her knees to her chest.

"Can we talk?" she asked quietly.

"Aw shit. What I do? You 'bout to break up with me already and I ain't even told you we go together yet."

Rue giggled and pulled him up so that he was sitting next to her. "I want you to hear exactly what I'm saying and don't add anything or make assumptions."

"Aight, wassup?"

"Sex with you wasn't what I was expecting. I didn't really have a lot of expectations since we just met, but it wasn't like... an emotional connection between us at all."

He processed her words before asking, "Did you not enjoy yourself?"

"No, it's not that. I did enjoy myself a lot. You made me cum... a lot. Like, what I experienced with you, that's never happened before."

"Then what's the problem?"

"It's just... We have different objectives, I guess. For you, there was no emotion, no intimacy. You only cared about getting to the destination. I love the journey. The kisses, the foreplay, the long, slow strokes..."

"And I prefer straight up fucking."

Rue chuckled nervously. "Yes. I know we're not in love, so I don't expect you to make love to me. I just... want to feel like there's more to what we're doing than just swapping cum. And I know there will be vibes where all I want is straight up nasty fucking. I just don't want that all the time."

Gotti didn't feel offended. He knew by the fluids released from her body that she *thoroughly* enjoyed herself. If he couldn't please a woman in any other way, Gotti knew how to please a woman sexually. He made it his priority. The wetter their pussy was, the better it felt for him.

He hadn't, however, cared about the emotional or mental exchange. He didn't kiss while he fucked. Just at the beginning. No missionary. No talking. Damn sure no declarations of love.

Rue was challenging him in a lot of ways in a short amount of time, and if Gotti was honest with himself, he liked that shit.

"I respect that, and I hear you." His voice relaxed when he asked, "Can we try again?"

"You really want to? Because I don't want to change you. You're crazy but I like you just as you are."

Gotti chuckled. "I like you, too, and seeing as I don't say that often, I'm willing to try."

"Okay," she agreed sheepishly before covering her eyes as if she was shy.

"Don't get shy on me now. I'm 'bout to bust that pussy open again."

"Gotti..."

"I'ma do it softly."

Her eyes rolled as she smiled. "Ooh, look at you initiating a kiss," she teased against his lips, making him laugh.

She made him do that a lot.

"Shut up and kiss me."

They kissed, and kissed, and kissed. And touched. And caressed. And licked. And nibbled. There was no part of her body that Gotti hadn't acquainted himself with, and she'd done the same to him. When he slipped his hand between her legs and felt how wet she was, he was blown away.

"Oh, so that's the difference?"

"Mhm," she moaned, chest heaving as she looked at him with lust-lowered eyes. "That's the difference."

Gotti laid her flat on the bed and made his way between her legs. He took his time feasting on her pussy, which was something he didn't do often. Quite frankly, there was no need. Women in his past were wet just at the thought of fucking him. And even if he did want them wetter, he used his hands.

Rue's pussy was decadent. From the first swipe of his tongue, Gotti was addicted. After she came the first time and he didn't stop, he realized he was eating her pussy for his pleasure, not for hers. Her legs trembled as she struggled to keep her eyes open. When her head flung back, she warned him that she was about to cum again. Only then did he lift himself, and that was just because his dick was getting jealous.

He wanted to feel Rue too.

Gotti tried to get out of bed to grab a condom, but she stopped him. She switched their positions, giving him eye contact and sloppy head that had his mind gone. Her moans as she sucked and stroked him fueled his ego. He wasn't a vocal lover in the past, especially from head, but Rue's head was different. It was like she had him under a spell. Gotti didn't have control over his body. He came far quicker than he wanted to and didn't give a damn about it.

He made his way over to his dresser and grabbed two condoms. Momentarily, he stopped walking. The sight of her in his bed... She looked like that was where she belonged. Shaking the thought from his head, he started back toward the bed. Rue spread her legs, and he moaned. She patted her glistening pussy and told him, "Come right here, baby."

"Damn, bae. You wet as hell. Let me eat it one more time."

"Gotti, I wan—mmm..." Her words were replaced with a moan when his mouth wrapped around her clit. When he played with her nipples, she wrapped her legs around his neck and confessed, "My nipples are so sensitive. If you don't stop, I'm going to cum."

He twirled them then tugged them and repeated the motion, causing her to cum again. Bypassing the condoms, he slid up her body and pressed his way inside of her.

"Gotti," she whispered before panting.

A growl escaped him as he throbbed inside of her. That certainly wasn't a part of the plan. "The fuck?"

She hummed and wrapped her arms and legs around him. "Stay present with me. Don't be scared."

His forehead rested on hers as he pulled out and stroked her slowly. "You making me fall in love with you, girl."

"Is that such a bad thing?"

Was it?

It used to feel like it... but not with her.

"I ain't never been in love before," he confessed. "You gon' have to teach me how to love you."

Rue cupped his cheeks and looked into his eyes as hers watered. "I will if you teach me how to love you."

His head shook as he looked toward the ceiling. If she kept that shit up, she'd turn him into a minute man. The slow missionary, the mindfulness, the eye contact, the kisses —it was all new to Gotti, but something he wanted to experience again and again. Being in the moment with her— witnessing the change in her breathing, her body trembling, the tightening of her walls... signs of her climax... it all made him hyperaware.

For the first time in his life, sex wasn't just about a nut. For the first time in his life, he felt physically, mentally, emotionally, and spiritually connected to another human being. For the first time in his life, he felt one with a woman.

"Ooh fuck," she slurred, reaching up and grabbing the headboard. "Oh shit. Oh—I'm—I—" Rue released a sizzling breath before she convulsed underneath him.

Gotti moaned as he picked her up and rocked her against him as she clung to him tightly. Their lips connected as he picked up to a medium pace. The wetter she got, the harder it was for him not to cum. He knew he only had one left in him, and he wanted to make it last.

"Gotti," she whimpered, holding the back of his head. "You ca-can't give this dick to nobody else. Me, me, j-just for me," Rue slurred as her walls squeezed him.

"It's all yours, bae. *I'm* all yours."

His declaration made her gush and squirt against him. "Fuck!" he roared, pulling out of her pulsing walls to avoid cumming. Gotti chuckled as he laid her on the bed. "I don't want this shit to end," he confessed, rolling her over onto her side.

"We can do it again," she reminded him as she grabbed his shaft and put him back inside.

"Mm... it's like that?"

"Yes, baby. I want you to fuck me now."

"You sure?"

"Mhm. I want you to fuck this pussy and cum."

That was all Gotti needed to hear. He gripped her waist and filled her with swift, hard strokes from behind. When he felt himself reaching his peak, he bit her neck, and that sent her over the edge. They came together, and Gotti came harder than he ever had in his life.

They rolled over onto their backs, and Gotti stared at the ceiling as he regulated his breathing.

"How was that?" he asked.

"Perfect. How soon can we do it again?"

25

R^{ue} Two Days Later

RUE HAD STAYED BEHIND TO WORK ON SECURING THE real estate developer with Gotti. After that, they decided to go and have drinks to celebrate. As she put the files in order, she asked Gotti to get the key to the file cabinet out of her purse.

"Hell nah. I don't go in women's purses. I'ma just bring it to you."

"That's fine," she said through her chuckle.

When he set her purse down it opened, allowing him to see the Plan B box inside.

"You not on birth control?" he asked.

"No, but don't worry, I took them."

"Cool."

She was surprised he didn't blow up about it, sure he'd

accuse her of wanting to trap him with a baby. After she locked the files up, she asked, "That's all? Cool?"

Gotti shrugged. "Yeah. What else you want me to say?"

"I don't know. I guess I'm just surprised you trust me."

"We exchanged STD results on the way to the hotel that first night. If I didn't trust you, I wouldn't have fucked you raw."

That was true, so she didn't press it. "I guess that just reminds me that we don't really know each other and have a lot to talk about. We vibe really well and the attraction is there, but not all the facts."

"They'll come with time. I'm invested as long as you are."

She smiled and rounded her desk to walk over to him. "I am too."

"Good." After dropping a kiss to her lips, he told her, "Let's get out of here before I risk them pills and fuck you again."

"I mean... You wouldn't get any complaints from me, but I'm hungry, so let's go."

Gotti chuckled as they walked out of her office. "Wanna go shopping?" he asked, checking the time on his Rolex.

"Do I want to go shopping?" she repeated.

"Yeah."

"Uh, sure."

"Aight where?"

Confused by his question, Rue looked around as if the answer would magically appear. "The mall?"

Gotti laughed as he scratched his nostril. "Which mall?"

"The one downtown I guess."

"You can go to literally any mall you want, and you choose a mall here?"

"Oh. I mean... I didn't... you were asking... We can travel?"

"Yeah. We just brought a major client back and I want to celebrate. Plus, I wanna spoil you a lil. So where you wanna go?"

Her heart squeezed at his words. "I don't know, Gotti," she almost whispered, avoiding his eyes. "I love shopping in Atlanta and Houston."

"Aight, so we'll do both. Where else you wanna go?"

Her eyes returned to his. "You're serious, aren't you?"

"Dead. Once we get the plans together, I'll secure the jet for tomorrow. We can stay for as long as you want." Gotti wrapped his arms around her. "Close your eyes, and tell me your perfect day."

Rue grinned as she considered the possibilities. "Brunch at the Tiffany & Co. restaurant in New York. Blue Box Café. Shopping in Atlanta. Self-care and spa time in Scottsdale or Sedona. A great dinner and then ending the night dancing and singing in Miami or Vegas."

"Seeing as Miami and Vegas are two of my favorite cities, I think we just became best friends. Let's do it."

"Really?" she asked through her laugh.

"Really. You down?"

"Yes!" she squealed, jumping into his arms. Gotti laughed softly as he held her close. Rue was still reeling over what was happening between them, but for once in her life, she would let loose and go with the flow.

———

Five Days Later

B. Love

WHAT WAS SUPPOSED TO BE ONE OR TWO DAYS AWAY turned into five, and Rue had no complaints. On the jet ride to their first destination, they shared the facts about themselves. She shared with him that she came from a two parent household and had a sister who was married with a son. Her parents were still alive and married and awaiting their arrival for Chalupa's funeral. Because of her spontaneous trip, they changed the date.

Gotti shared facts about himself and his family too. He didn't tell her a lot about the cartel. Just that it was a major part of himself and that he took pride in what he was. Who he was. She wouldn't deny the thrill and excitement but also expressed her safety concerns. Gotti was honest with her about the risks and told her he'd do everything to make sure that part of his life never negatively affected her.

The SUV that was full of her shopping bags was on its way to Rose Valley Hills. Gotti had already made plans to have it delivered to her penthouse apartment. She enjoyed being with a man that made plans and was proactive, allowing her to relax and cut her brain off for a change.

As they cruised the Memphis streets he asked her, "Why *Nahtahn Designs*? You're bomb at what you do. How'd you get into it?"

"I always admired your mother's work. She was used as an example while I was in school. I interned for her when I was in college, and she mentored me." Rue took his hand into hers. "I really cared about her. She was truly special to me."

Gotti looked over at her briefly. "That means a lot. I'm sure she felt the same about you. Mommy didn't let a lot of people in, like me, but when she did, you were in for life." He released a shaky breath. "So what's the goal for you? Are you content being the head of design for the next ten or twenty years?"

"Not at all." She giggled as she looked out of the window. "Don't get me wrong, I love what I do, but I want to do something new. I love administrative work and shepherding. Ideally, I'd want my own design firm or to be CEO of *Nahtahn Designs*. And I'm not saying that because things are personal between us. If I ever were to get that position, I want it to be because I'm the best person for the job."

"I feel you."

Their conversation shifted directions again. By the time they made it to her parents' neighborhood, they were talking about how they wanted to be loved and their love languages, though Gotti didn't believe in that term and having just one, and what they had to offer.

"What's one thing you need from me for this to be a successful relationship?" he asked.

"Provision. Not just monetary. I need you to provide security, stability, partnership, openness. A safe space for me to be a woman. Your woman."

"I can do that, but if I ever feel like I can't, I promise to let you know."

Rue appreciated his honesty. "What's one thing you need from me?"

"I need you to see me. Accept me. If you can do that, everything else can be handled with time."

"Mm, I love that. I think a lot of people aren't seen in their relationships. That's why they don't feel loved." She chuckled as she reminisced. "I remember I was dating this guy and he wasn't sentimental at all. He was thoughtless. I could literally tell him what I wanted, and he didn't do it. One year for Christmas, all I asked him for was a love letter. Instead, he bought me a car. He got so mad that I didn't want the car. I genuinely just wanted something I could read again and again to know how he felt about me."

As she sighed, Gotti said, "I assume y'all broke up shortly after that."

"Yeah, that night. To this day his narrative is that I wasn't grateful." She cleared her throat and looked out the window. "Said all that to say, I would love to see you for all that you are. For who you are."

Gotti gripped her thigh, and when she looked at him, he leaned against the center console and kissed her.

The closer they got to the house, the more somber her mood became. By the time they pulled up, she'd grown completely silent. Though she hated having to say goodbye to Chalupa, she felt peace having Gotti by her side.

26

G otti
Late March

THOUGH HE COULD HAVE EASILY DRIVEN HER, GOTTI didn't mind walking Rue home from work. It was only five minutes away from the office. He understood her desire to walk instead of riding in a car because of the accident, so when things were nearby, walking was an easy compromise. As they walked silently, hand in hand, Gotti considered asking if she wanted to meet his family. Him meeting hers was more out of necessity than anything else because of her dog's funeral. He wasn't sure if she would have wanted him to meet them so soon otherwise. They'd only been dating for a couple of weeks, and though it felt like a lifetime, things were moving pretty fast.

"Rue!" At the sound of someone calling her name, Gotti tightened his grip on her hand.

"You know him?"

She exhaled a hard breath. "That's my ex Alex."

"So this who you cheating on me with?" Alex roared as he stormed over to them.

With no hesitation, Gotti pulled his Glock, and it stopped Alex's movement. With the gun in the center of Alex's forehead, Gotti said, "I don't know who the fuck you are, but you better back the fuck up unless you want me to make you look like Swiss cheese."

"You gon' let him talk to your man like that?" Alex asked, looking around Gotti to Rue as she stood behind him. "Who is this nigga anyway?"

"I'm not going to say it again," Gotti warned.

"Please go, Alex. We're not together, but I don't want to see you get hurt."

Alex's eyes squinted. When he shifted his attention from Rue and really focused on Gotti he smiled and took a step back.

"I'll be seeing you, Rue," he said as he walked away.

"You gon' be seeing God if you come around my girl again, nigga. And that's on my ma."

The only reason Gotti didn't pull the trigger then was because he didn't want Rue to see that side of him. Not yet.

"Gotti, please," she called softly, placing her hand on his arm, but Gotti didn't lower it until Alex was a safe distance away. He didn't get the vibe that he was a threat at all, but he didn't like the aggression he approached Rue with. Gotti also didn't like the delusion he had thinking Rue was still his.

Gotti waited until they were in her apartment to ask, "Who was he?"

"My ex, Alex. We broke up a while ago, but he can't let it go."

"Is he stalking you, or was him being here tonight a coincidence?"

"I wouldn't say he's stalking me, but he does pop up every once in a while to try and get me back."

She avoided his eyes and played with her fingers in that same way Kayla did when she was nervous.

"He ever put his hands on you?" When her head hung, Gotti chuckled. "I'm going to kill him."

"Please don't. He never hit me with his fist. It was just... like... a choke or slap or push when we were arguing."

"So!" he yelled, and when she jumped, he felt like shit.

Gotti wasn't expecting her to break into tears, and he felt worse thinking it was because of him. He hesitated on whether or not he should try and console her, but that seemed like the right thing to do. He'd rather she push him away than feel like she couldn't trust him to be there for her. Risking it, Gotti closed the space between them and wrapped his arms around her.

"I'm sorry for yelling at you, Rue. I'm used to you being my lil chihuahua. I didn't mean to hurt your feelings."

She laughed softly through her sniffle. "I'm not crying because of you. I'm crying because of this situation. I hate that I even met him. Loving him blinded me and made me deal with things I knew were wrong. If I wasn't so blind, I would have burned his dick the first time he cheated and had my cousins whup his ass the first time he slapped me." She sighed and buried her face against Gotti.

"Uh, you said... burned his..." Gotti cleared his throat, making her snicker. "It don't matter. I wouldn't cheat on you anyway."

"Good, because your dick is too good to be punished for your indiscretions."

167

"I hear the smile in your voice, but I also know your ass crazy, so I'ma take heed to the warning."

Rue laughed as he kissed her head, and the gentle gesture put her even more in her feelings. "I'm just exhausted from dealing with him, baby, and I want him to leave me alone."

"I will make that happen."

"I don't want you to kill him, Gotti. Seriously. I don't want that on my conscience. Promise me you won't kill him."

Gotti huffed as his head shook. "Nah, man. I can't e'en lie to you like that."

"Gotti, *please.*" Rue pulled herself off his chest and took his hands into hers. "He's a member of the RVG. If you go after him, they will retaliate. I don't want you having to deal with that because of me."

Gotti was aware of the Rose Valley Gang. They weren't a gang that the Nahtahn Cartel supplied or had an interest in partnering with. They weren't worth the connect. More than anything, they were young hoodlums causing the city pain and damage. Last Gotti heard, the six men Gambino gunned down outside of *Lamar's Fish Shack* last year were members of the gang. They had been tearing Lamar's neighborhood up. They were menaces, true bullies, and Gotti was struggling to understand how she was with someone like Alex if she initially had a problem with him. Then again, people often didn't show their true colors until you were comfortable with them.

"You clearly don't know who I am to think I give a fuck about him or his little ass gang."

"That's not what I mean, baby." She cupped his cheeks and lowered him to her, pecking his lips three times. "I know you're more than capable of handling him and protecting me. What I'm saying is, they will retaliate. I don't want to cause you any problems."

"It would never be a problem to protect the woman I'm falling in love with. I won't have peace if I don't do something about this. He could pop up at any time, and knowing you walk a lot, it would eat at me thinking he caught you and..." His head shook as if he was unable to even say the words.

"I understand," she muttered. "Can we compromise?"

Gotti considered her words. "I will try to talk to him once to make sure he understands what will happen if he doesn't leave you alone. If he comes around here again, I'm going to kill him, and I won't give a fuck *what* you say."

"Okay," she agreed, putting space between them. Already, Gotti hated the disconnect. It made him question if she could truly handle being with a man like him. While he understood her desire to not bring him any drama, that wasn't her responsibility. It was taking everything inside of him not to go after Alex. He lived for this shit. It wasn't on him; it was truly in him. Gotti would bleed Alex and every member of RVG dry before he let them come between him and the best woman he'd ever had.

The Next Afternoon

"WHAT ARE YOU IN THE MOOD FOR?" RUE ASKED, walking into Gotti's office with her head buried in her iPad. "I know you usually want my pussy for lunch, but I mean actual food."

Gambino cleared his throat, and Rue's head lifted. At

the sight of both of his brothers, she dropped her iPad. "Oh shit. Sorry."

"Rue," Gotti called, but she was too busy scurrying out of his office to respond.

Gambino and Luciano waited until she was gone to laugh.

"Aight, so clearly you fucked her," Gambino said.

"Which is no surprise," Luciano added.

"Nah, don't even go there with her. It's more than just sex, for real."

Both brothers held a serious expression as they looked at him.

"You like her?" Gambino confirmed.

"I'm falling in love with her. That's actually why I asked y'all to meet me here today."

They listened intently as he explained what happened last night with her ex. When he was done, Gotti said, "Now I'm tryna handle this the right way. I tracked him down, but I didn't go after him. I want y'all to set up an official meeting between us and the RVG chief so he will know this shit is real. He only has one chance to stay the fuck away from Rue before I bury him, and I'm firm on that shit."

Luciano and Gambino looked at each other. Gambino was the first to speak.

"The fact that she convinced you to think before you act says a lot. She already solid in my book. I'll set the meeting up."

"Now go get ya lil freak so we can make sure she good," Luciano said with a grin, causing all three brothers to laugh.

Gotti stood and walked next door to Rue's office. She was pacing and chewing her thumb nail. Gotti smiled as he wrapped his arms around her from behind and rocked from side to side to soothe her.

"My fault, bae. I should have told you they were here since you came in late."

"Ya think! I am *so* embarrassed."

"Why?" he asked with a laugh.

"I don't want that to be their first impression of me. Oh my God. They probably think I'm a freak."

"Ain't nothing wrong with that."

"Gotti!" she whisper-yelled, and he laughed.

"Come on, lil stink. I'ma introduce you before they go. I didn't want you to meet them this way, but I did want you to meet them. Only person missing is my sis."

Rue turned in his arms. "You want me to meet your family?"

"Yeah. I meant it when I said I was falling in love with you. I ain't taking this shit lightly."

Her hands slid up and down his arms as her bottom lip poked out slightly. Even standing on the tips of her toes, there was a significant height difference, so Gotti lowered himself to kiss her. That kiss led to him sitting her on the edge of her desk.

"Baby, we can't. The door window..."

"I'on give a fuck about that shit." As he pulled his dick out, he asked, "You want what I got for you, or nah?"

Her hand stroked him as she licked her lips. "Give it to me."

As he put her ankles on his shoulders, Rue pushed her panties to the side. Slowly, he stretched her walls. Her chin trembled and eyes fluttered as she fought to not moan.

"I ain't never had no pussy like this," he confessed, stroking her slowly.

"Gotti, please," she begged.

"Please what?"

The office was silent except for her shallow breathing

171

and wetness coating him. Her legs trembled as she struggled to stay quiet. When Gotti pressed her legs against her chest and stroked her faster, she moaned and grabbed his wrists as they gripped her desk.

"Oh my God, baby. I can't take it. Not without getting loud."

"Then finish for me so I can cum."

Her legs trembled and dangled from his ankles. Head flung back, Rue whimpered his praises. He was so mesmerized by her, he was in no rush to cum at all. The only reason he teased her clit was because his brothers were waiting.

Rue's legs wrapped around him, and she kept him close, forcing him to go deep. Their eyes remained locked until she neared her peak. Gotti bit down on her shoulder, because apparently, being bitten made her cum harder. His hand wrapped around her mouth just in time to muffle her choppy moans, but Gotti knew there was still a chance that his brothers heard her. At that point, he didn't even care as he came.

Once his heart settled down, he pulled out, and they went to the bathrooms to get cleaned up. Holding her hand, Gotti led her into his office. He wasn't sure how his face looked, but Gambino chuckled and shook his head when he saw him.

"Aight, this my lil chihuahua Rue," he introduced, swatting her fist when she swung at him.

"You just couldn't resist calling me that, could you?"

"Chihuahua?" Luciano repeated as both brothers stood to embrace her. "Do we even want to know what that's about?"

"Well, at first it was because that was what she was acting like when she was mad the day we met. Ironically, she had a chihuahua that she look—ow!" Gotti rubbed his arm where she'd pinched him. "Stop pinching me. Yo' lil boney ass fingers hurt."

After their laughter settled, Gambino offered to take her to lunch so they could get to know her better, which Gotti appreciated. He was even happier when Kayla showed up...

27

R^{ue} April

A MONTH HAD PASSED, AND THINGS COULDN'T HAVE
been better for Rue. Things at *Nahtahn Designs* were better
than ever, her relationship with Gotti was blossoming, and
her sister would be coming to visit her soon. She wasn't sure
what Gotti had said or done, but she hadn't heard a peep
out of Alex and was grateful for that.

As she headed out of her apartment, she called Ashley
to make sure they were still on for coffee to catch up. Gotti
had been taking up so much of her time that she felt like she
hadn't seen her best friend in ages. Ashley didn't care,
because she'd been cozying up with her new boo too. It was
Gotti's cousin Hampton. They met two weeks ago when the
family gathered to celebrate all the hard work Gotti had
been doing. She loved to see her man be celebrated, because
she knew how much being seen meant to him.

"Hey, best friend," Ashley answered as always.

"Hey, pooh. I just wanted to make sure we were still on for coffee this morning."

"We are. I'm parking in front of *Booked & Brewed* now."

"Okay, perfect. I'm walking out, so I'll see you in a few minutes."

"Okay, cool."

Rue hummed with a content smile on her face. She saw the flowers on the front desk, but she didn't think they were for her. When Taylor called her over and told her she had a package, warmth spread through her chest. Rue almost skipped over to the desk. She inhaled the scent of the flowers and marveled at the diamond choker before asking Taylor to help her put it on. Her movements grew still when she saw what looked to be a handwritten letter from Gotti. After asking Taylor to put the flowers in the refrigerator until she made it home for the day, Rue headed outside as she read the letter.

My lil chihuahua,

I know words mean a lot to you. Thoughtful-ness. Consideration. Sentiment. All that shit. That's not me organically, but I'm working on it, because you're worth it. We're worth it. I ain't ever had a woman to make me feel the way you do. You make me feel seen, heard, and valued. I feel safe with you. You increase my peace. You challenge me to be better. To be

*layered. I have fun with you, and I want to
spend the rest of my life with you. It seem
kinda corny telling you I love you for the first
time in a letter, so I'll tell you when I see
you later at work today.*

Your baby,
Gotti

HOLDING THE NOTE TO HER CHEST, RUE TRIED TO
blink back her tears. She never thought things would have
progressed between them the way they had, but she
wouldn't deny that she loved him too. Rue was so caught up
in the warm feelings the letter produced that she didn't see
Alex behind her... but she felt him.

The sharp blow he sent to the back of her head caused
her to see stars as her ears rang. She fell forward, and the
letter blew from her hand.

"My chief sat me down for a month because of yo'
nigga," he said against your ear. "Give him this message for
me," was the last thing Rue heard before a second hit
knocked her out.

28

Gotti

Gotti stared at Rue's desk. She was late. Usually if she was going to be late, she would call him. He checked the time on his Rolex again, trying to remember if she'd mentioned being late and he just forgot. She did say she was grabbing coffee with Ashley. Maybe she lost track of time. Before he could call her again, her desk phone rang, and for some reason, Gotti's heart dropped into the pit of his stomach.

He answered it with, "Yes?"

"Mr. Nahtahn, I have Ashley on line three for Ms. Williams. Is she in yet?"

"No, but I'll take the call."

"Yes, sir. Please hold."

A few seconds passed before the call connected. "Ashley? Rue isn't with you?"

"No. I was calling to see if she'd maybe gone straight to work and couldn't text me. I've been calling her, and she hasn't answered."

"Something is wrong," he said more to himself than her. "I'm about to go to her apartment."

"Okay. I'll meet you there."

"Aight."

Gotti disconnected the call and stalked down the hall. He didn't feel like answering a million questions from his brothers, so instead, he sent them a 911 text and Rue's address. His gut was telling him Alex was responsible for whatever happened, and he'd better damn well pray he had time to leave the city before Gotti caught him if he valued his fucking life.

At the Hospital

"STAY CALM," KAYLA SAID, GRABBING GOTTI'S HAND. She was with Gambino finalizing some things for their wedding when Gotti texted them. "She's going to need you levelheaded. Stay calm."

Gotti released a shaky breath as he looked at Kayla. He heard what she was saying, but he couldn't make any guarantees, because he didn't know what he was about to walk into. When he got to the apartment, Rue was nowhere in sight, but the doorman told him what happened. The police were still there taking witness statements and looking at camera footage from the corner camera. When he saw Alex attack her, Gotti saw red. He told the detective they better find Alex before he did.

When he stepped into her room, tears immediately

pooled in Rue's eyes. White bandage was wrapped around her head and there were small scratches on her cheek. From the video, it looked like Alex was only able to hit her twice before the doorman and security came rushing out. Both hits were to the back of the head.

Gotti climbed into bed with her, and she immediately began to cry. It took everything inside of Gotti not to shed tears over her pain. As he held her, he closed his eyes and willed his tears not to fall.

"I'ma kill 'em all," he promised. "Every last fuckin' one of 'em."

"Let me get her doctor for an update," Gambino said.

Gotti didn't register the words. All he heard were Rue's sniffles. All he felt were her hands clinging to him for dear life.

When her doctor arrived, he shared that she did have a concussion and minor scrapes and bruises from her fall. He hesitated before sharing the news, and Rue nodded for him to continue. Gotti thought he was hearing things when Dr. Daniels said their baby was fine.

"Baby?" he repeated.

"I think it happened that day I met your brothers. I forgot to get a Plan B. I'm sorry."

That time, Gotti was unable to stop his tears. She wiped them away but more came.

"Awww, baby brother!" Kayla cooed, wrapping her arms around him and kissing his cheek. "Congratulations, sis," she said, leaning across the bed and hugging and kissing Rue until she giggled.

"Wow. My baby brother about to have a baby. I can't believe it," Gambino said, pulling Gotti out of the bed for an embrace. "Congratulations, Gotti. You know we got you every step of the way. My niece or nephew 'bout to be spoiled as *fuck*."

"My baby," Luciano said, pulling his youngest brother in for a hug. "I give you hell because I want more for you, and it seems you got it. You know I love you and every extension of you. Congratulations, baby brother."

Gotti's tears finally dried as the weight of being a father settled within him. He thanked his family before making his way over to Rue.

"How do you feel?" he asked, taking her hands into his.

"Scared but excited. How do you feel?"

"You having my baby. I'm happier than a muthafucka."

They all laughed as Rue's eyes watered. "I love you too," she muttered, cupping his cheek. "I think my letter blew away after he... but I love you too."

"That don't even matter. I'm just glad you're okay. I'll write you a letter every day if that's what you want. I love you."

He gave her a hug and kiss, but suddenly, Gotti was even more determined to end Alex's life. He refused to let him get anywhere near Rue, especially now that she was pregnant with his baby.

They waited until Ashley and Rue's parents arrived to leave, and Gotti promised he'd be back before she had time to miss him. Alex wasn't hard to find. He was the cocky type who posted his location on social media.

After they loaded the teams and their guns, they headed to *Lamar's Fish Shack*. From Alex's last post, him and a few members of RVG were hanging out smoking and drinking on the corner in front of it. For the entire drive, Gotti remained silent. Nothing needed to be said. His brother's understood how important it was to handle the threat, and they were down for him and willing to do whatever to make that happen.

Normally, the Nahtahn Cartel didn't shoot when innocent bystanders were around. That night, as far as Gotti was concerned, *anybody* could fucking get it. After killing the lights on the SUV, they pulled up with a slow creep. Automatic rifles pointed out of the windows, making targets out of Alex and everyone that was sitting with him as bystanders scattered. When the gunfire ceased, Gotti hopped out of the SUV. He checked Alex's pockets for the diamond choker he'd snatched from Rue's neck and sent a kick to his head before spitting on him and turning to leave.

Gotti thanked his people before they went their separate ways. He went home long enough to shower and pick up a few things that were out of place, because Rue was coming home with him when she was discharged, and he wouldn't take no for an answer.

When he made his way back to the hospital, she was fast asleep. Gotti put the choker around her neck and climbed into bed with her. His hand rested on her belly, and she stirred slightly before nestling against him and falling into a deeper sleep.

29

R ue
One Week Later

RUE WAS ON A CLOUD. GOTTI HAD BASICALLY MOVED
her into his home in Nahtahn Cove, and she was more
than okay with that. Her parents hovered over her for a
while, but eventually, they felt safe going back home to
Memphis when they heard about what happened to
Alex. Neither seemed to have the courage to ask Gotti if
he was responsible, but Rue suspected they knew
he was.

That weekend, she'd have a girls' trip with her sister
Melanie, Ashley, and Kayla. Kayla had become like another
big sister to Rue, and she was grateful for the connection.
Gambino and Luciano had been waiting on her hand and
foot since she arrived, though she assured them she was
okay. She had no idea how they would act when she was
further along in her pregnancy. To see large, powerful,

brutal men act soft and gentle toward her always tickled her.

All in all, life was great, and Rue was convinced nothing would make it better. Finally feeling confident enough to return to work, Rue busied herself with getting ready for the day. Breakfast was being prepared by their private chef, and Rue was looking forward to eating with Gotti. He'd be leaving *Nahtahn Designs* next month, and the moment would be bittersweet.

Even with them living together, she'd gotten used to working with him and would miss his presence. The only good thing about him leaving was that she'd be the permanent CEO, and Rue prayed every day she was there that she'd make Claire proud.

When Rue heard what she thought was the sound of pitter patter against the tile, she stopped fluffing her curls. With a shrug, she continued to get herself together until she heard what sounded like an excited dog sneeze. Leaving the master bathroom, her knees grew weak at the sight of three chihuahua puppies. Covering her mouth, she immediately started to cry. Gotti wore a comfortable smile as he picked them up and walked over to her.

"Baby," she whined. "These are ours?"

"Yeah. I know they won't replace Chalupa but..."

"Aww, I love them already. And I love you!"

She hugged him and kissed him as much as the puppies pressed between them would allow.

"I love you, too, chihuahua. Now you got some mo' lil chihuahuas to play with."

Rue laughed as her eyes rolled playfully. "I'm so happy I don't even care about that. Thank you! Give them to me."

Gotti chuckled as she sat down and put all three puppies in her lap.

"What?" she asked when his expression turned serious.

"Nothing just..." Gotti's head shook. She reached for his hand and sat him next to her. "I know Mommy would've loved seeing me love you."

"She sees it," Rue assured him before giving him a soft kiss. "And she sees me loving the hell out of you too."

They shared another brief kiss before the puppies climbing up her chest gained her attention.

She giggled incessantly and cried happy tears as their little tails wagged while they gave her kisses. Her eyes locked with Gotti's, and she thanked God for him.

Who knew the softest, safest love could come from a thug?

The Future

30

L uciano Nahtahn
That Fall

ALL WAS WELL WITHIN THE NAHTAHN CARTEL.

Gambino and Kayla had just gotten married in Puerto Vallarta. Gotti and Rue were going strong, and they were set to learn the sex of their baby in four weeks. Business was booming, and their partnership with the Russian mafia led to Gambino considering working with other families as well. *Nahtahn Designs* was bringing in twice the profit since Gotti took over, and Luciano was confident it would continue to grow in Rue's capable hands.

With things between Gambino and Cory being healthy, he agreed to stay on permanently as his consigliere. That meant Gotti was able to become underboss after rightfully earning it, and Luciano was who and what he always wanted to be—enforcer and head of security.

As Luciano sipped his champagne, his eyes scanned the

room. Even though it was only family and friends at the wedding reception, he was trained to always be alert. Gambino made his way over with a syrupy grin and glossy eyes—indicators of his inebriation. Gambino had been working hard, and he deserved to let loose and enjoy himself. After their customary temple kiss and embrace, Gambino spoke.

"In six weeks, I need you to go to LA and talk to the head of the Colombian cartel out there. I want him to push our supply. Make that happen, regardless of what it takes. His reach in the west coast is massive. If we can supply him and Delgado in Vegas, we'll take over the west and be heavy on every coast."

"I'll handle it, but why can't you go? I feel like he would be more receptive to you."

Gambino's expression saddened as he looked around to make sure no one was coming toward them.

"Me and kitten got an appointment that week. She's been off her birth control for a while now and is stressing over not being pregnant by now."

"It happens in its own time."

"You and I know that, but she's too emotional to be logical about it."

"So what... She thinks something's wrong?"

"Yeah. Apparently when we first broke up all those years ago, she was pregnant and lost the baby, so she feels like that has something to do with it. We went to her regular gynecologist, and they told her she was healthy and that they saw nothing that would prevent her from getting pregnant, but she still wants to go see a specialist."

"Damn. I'm sorry to hear that, brotha. I'm confident it'll happen, though, but I'll handle that meeting for you."

"I 'preciate you. I'll have Cory get with you and let you

know everything you need to know. But let me get back to my wife before she figures out I'm talking business."

Luciano laughed as his brother walked away. His eyes landed on Gotti as he sang the Kem song that was playing to Rue as they danced. She was glowing, and Gotti was happier and healthier than he'd ever been.

All was well within the Nahtahn family.

The only thing that would make it better was when Luciano found a love of his own. There was no rush for that, though, because he understood with the changes in both of his brothers' lives that someone would have to have the freedom and flexibility to handle business when their wives and children came first. The meeting he'd have to attend in six weeks was proof of that.

As Luciano downed the last of his champagne, his focus zeroed in on Tori—his private chef. She was a milk chocolate hued goddess that he'd been wanting to melt on his tongue since she started working for him five years ago. Though they were flirtatious with each other at times, things always remained professional. He felt trapped under her spell as she glided in his direction. She stood next to him at the bar, smelling edible as vanilla and honey wafted from her pores.

"I have a trip in six weeks to LA. Make sure you're available to travel," he told her.

Tori smiled. "I was hoping since Bino invited me to his wedding that meant I was finally in the family and this wasn't a work trip."

"If it isn't... What you wanna do?"

"Why don't you bring my drink to my room and find out?"

Luciano's eyes were trained on her ass and hips swaying as she walked away. The size sixteen beauty could sit on his face *any*-fucking-day. After grabbing her drink and a glass of tequila for himself, Luciano headed to her beach house that was just steps away from the party on the sandy beach restaurant patio. He slid the glass door open and stepped inside. As Tori dropped the strings of her maxi dress, she looked back at him over her shoulder with a smile.

Maybe love wasn't too far away after all...

31

T ori
Six Weeks Later
Mid-September

TORI WAS EXCITED TO SEE HER BROTHER, BUT SHE WAS still on edge. He wanted to meet in a sketchy neighborhood that was known for its crime. The crazy thing was, it was just a few blocks from where Tori and Juan grew up. She lived there from birth to the age of eighteen. Ten years later, being near that part of the hood made her uncomfortable. While Tori wouldn't suggest she was rich... being the private chef for Luciano Nahtahn provided her with a nice lifestyle.

She was paid seven thousand dollars a month, had weekends off unless he was hosting a dinner or party, and lived in the mother-in-law suite behind his home at Nahtahn Cove. All of her bills were paid for by Luciano, and he made sure there was always a town car waiting to take her wherever she wanted to go. For that trip, though, she needed to drive herself, so Tori pulled out the Honda Accord that she took to the Cove years ago and drove maybe a handful of times a year ever since.

As she pulled into the gas station, her eyes rolled at the sight of a group of men by the door. Though she had no plans of getting out, she didn't even want them to notice her. Like the Kia boys in other cities, there was a group of young hoodlums in Rose Valley Hills stealing Hondas... even while people were in it. Tori quickly pulled into the back of the gas station by the trash compactor and hoped they hadn't seen her.

She called Juan, and her frustration grew when he didn't answer the call. Her half-brother had a way of making her love him more than anyone one second and loathing him the next. Tori's relationship with Juan had always been a love-hate relationship. Juan was two years older than her, and though he hated that her father stuck around and his didn't, eventually, he learned to love his sister and be her protector. Lately, it felt like their roles had been reversed.

Because of Juan's drug problem and her parents unwillingness to have anything to do with him until he was clean, he was always calling her to take care of and protect him. About six months had passed since the last time she'd heard from Juan, and though Tori wished it was because he was somewhere getting clean, the urgency in his voice when he asked her to meet him said otherwise.

Tori called his phone again, but she quickly ended the call when she saw a thin man speed walking toward her car. Upon first glance, she didn't think it was her brother. He was too tiny. The closer he got, the more she realized it was Juan. Covering her mouth, Tori gasped as her eyes watered. His eyes were dark and sunken in. Matted hair covered his head and face. His clothes were torn and dirty... and Tori wondered if it was because he'd been in a crack house smoking for God only knows how long or because he was homeless.

Taking a deep breath to compose herself, Tori's hand shook as she opened the door. She stepped out and immediately pulled her brother into her arms. Her tears threatened to pour when she felt his bones sticking out through his skin.

"Juan," she whispered, holding him tighter... afraid to let him go. "What are you *doing*, Juan?"

Juan pushed her back carefully, still holding her waist as he looked into her eyes. "I'm maintaining, baby sis," he said with a forced smile.

"It doesn't look like it. You're skin and bones." She looked his frame over before grabbing his face. "I can see your cheekbones, Juan. Your eyes... Let me feed you."

His head shook as he pushed her hands down from his face. "I'm good, Tor. I don't need food." He looked around nervously. "But I do need a few dollars if you can spare it. I owe someone and he's coming to collect tonight. If I don't have it, shit might get bad."

"Oh. Um... Okay." Tori opened the door and leaned across her seat to grab her purse from the passenger seat. She took the five hundred dollars she kept in cash from her wallet and stared at it as she told him, "This is all I have. Is five hundred enough?"

Relief washed over him as he quickly took the money and shoved it in his pocket. "That's enough, baby sis. Thank you. I gotta go." Juan placed a quick kiss to her cheek before jogging away.

For a few seconds, all she did was stare at him. She shouldn't have been, but a part of Tori was hurt that all he wanted from her after six months was money. Brushing that feeling off, she got back in her car and quickly swerved out of the gas station.

Tori was so in her head she didn't pay attention when she got home. Instead of going to the mother-in-law suite, she went into the main house. At the sight of Luciano in the sitting area sipping brown liquor, she jumped slightly.

"Sorry. I didn't know you were here."

"It's cool," he replied, eyes traveling her frame with no shame.

He'd been doing that ever since they slept together in Puerto Vallarta. For Tori, that trip was a chance for her to finally scratch her Luciano itch. She was surprised and honored when Gambino invited her to the wedding, because no one else on Luciano's or Gotti's staff were invited to come. It made her feel honored and seen as more than just the help. But when they all were on their way home, Tori and Luciano agreed what happened would be a onetime thing. That hadn't stopped him from looking at her as if he wanted to devour her every time they were in the same room though.

"Are you hungry?" she asked, looking at the time on the wall. "I can fix you something here before I go to the suite."

Luciano didn't respond right away. He finished his liquor and stood. She watched as his jaw clenched. Long, slow strides led him over to her.

Tori would never deny how attracted to Luciano she was. He was so tall and wide he made her look smaller than she actually was, and Tori loved being with a big man. Hell, Luciano was a big dawg. He didn't just look the part—he lived like one too. Caramel brown skin with a golden under-tone covered his thick build. His hair was cut low—almost bald. Pierced ears and two studs in his nose with a silver cross necklace were his everyday jewelry.

His lips and eyes were under turned, and he had a beard that she thoroughly enjoyed coating with her cum while they were in Mexico.

Luciano took her hands into his. "You're shaking. Tell me what's wrong so I can fix it."

His response was no surprise to her. That's what men like Luciano did. They fixed things. And when they couldn't, they fucked shit up.

"Nothing's wrong, I—"

"Don't fucking lie to me," he commanded through gritted teeth.

Pulling her hands out of his, Tori ran her fingers through her hair. She released a shaky breath as she headed toward the kitchen. Luciano followed behind. As she washed her hands, she told him, "I just saw my brother. I haven't talked to him in six months."

"Is he okay?"

"Depends on your definition. He's definitely still on drugs. I'm not sure what kind. He's done crack and heroin. I think he's on crack again."

"What did he want?"

Tori swallowed hard as she dried her hands. "Money. A part of me thought maybe he wanted to just... see me and catch up. I should have known that wouldn't be the case."

Her eyes watered and nostrils flared as she tried not to feel anything for her brother. She was tired of feeling for him. Tired of praying for and crying over him. Juan had been doing drugs since she was in high school. At first, it was just weed, but when someone put crack in it without telling him... *everything* changed. Over ten years had passed since Tori saw her brother sober for more than three weeks, and every time she saw him, he looked like a different version of himself.

"I'm sorry to hear that," Luciano said, pulling her into his arms for a hug Tori didn't realize she needed. "You need to be careful though. I know that's your brother and you love him, but you can't keep giving him money. The day you say no, you're going to see a version of your brother you've never seen before."

Tori didn't bother responding. As much as she didn't want to admit it, that was the truth.

32

L uciano
   In LA

THE FIRST THING TORI DID WHEN THEY ARRIVED WAS
put on her bathing suit and hop in the pool. Luciano set out
poolside, shades on, watching her every move. Now that
he'd finally tasted her and felt her walls... Luciano could
admit he wasn't wrapped as tight when it came to her. Up
until the wedding, he was able to downplay his desire
of her.

Like an addict, one kiss was all it took, and now... he was
hooked.

"You know I feel your eyes on me even though you have
on those shades, right?" she confirmed, gliding across the
water.

"The shades are not meant to hide the fact that I'm
looking."

She smiled. "That's what we're doing now? All work in The Hills but we play when we travel?"

"If that's what you wanna do. I'm cool with playing back at home too."

"Luciano..."

His eyes closed at the sound of her saying his name. People said his name all day, every day. But when Tori said it... it didn't just sound like his name. It sounded like a song, a chant, a sweet reminder of who he was and who she could have been to have that kind of power over him.

"Don't say my name like that unless you want me to give you a reason to."

She stood in the pool. Her curls stuck to her skin. "And how do I say your name... *Luciano*?"

Luciano chuckled and took a pull from his weed filled cigarillo. "Like you like it. Like you like *me*."

"What if I do?"

After Luciano downed the rest of his tequila on the rocks, he walked over to the pool. Tori squealed as he effortlessly picked her up out of the water. Their lips connected as he smacked her ass and carried her back over to his seat. As he pulled his dick out of his swim trunks, Tori lifted slightly and untied her bikini bottoms.

The moment he sat her down on his dick, it was like the piece of him that had been missing was returned. A low hum escaped her as she reached behind him and grabbed the pole of the large umbrella that granted them shade.

"Ride that dick and show me you missed it," Luciano ordered, untying her top. Her breasts bounced free, and he kneaded one while licking and sucking the other.

Her moans and wetness grew with each of his touches and commands. *Faster, harder, slow down, sit back, be still and let me fuck you.* Tori's arms wrapped around him as her movements grew sporadic.

"Luciano," she moaned, head tilting.

"I know you're about to cum. You look so fucking *pretty* when you do."

She moaned as her walls pulsed while she came. Luciano waited until she was done to have her stand up and lean against the glass table. Times like that made him glad he opted to stay at Airbnbs when they traveled alone. But with the way he was craving her, he would have fucked her even if others were around.

"Mhm," he moaned as he slipped inside of her from behind.

She rocked against him as he took a pull from the blunt. Luciano set it down then gripped her waist and fucked her hard and deep. He didn't mind when she was vocal, but his goal was to hit that spot that would leave her silent and breathless before she came. Arching her back further, he tilted himself and pressed against her spot.

"Ooh," she purred, gripping his thigh. Her moans turned into whimpers that turned into choppy breaths. Once Luciano was confident she was at her peak, he hardened his strokes and allowed his balls to tap her clit. "Yes, yes, yes!" she chanted as she came, gripping the table and his thigh for support.

He stroked her until he couldn't hold back, then pulled out and told her to swallow his seeds. Tori dropped to her knees and looked up at him with those dark, piercing eyes that he'd fallen in love with. She played with her ample breasts as her mouth hung open, ready to receive every drop of him.

"Fuck," Luciano growled as his body jerked. He gripped her head and fucked her mouth, moaning when she closed it and sucked him. Working his balls, she circled her neck in a way that had his toes curling. "Ahh, shit. You's a nasty lil—*fuck!*" When her tongue swirled under his shaft between it and his balls, Luciano shivered.

"Mmm," she purred before swallowing him whole until he came again.

When she'd emptied him, Tori stood and grabbed her bikini top. Luciano stood weakly as she pranced away. At the back door, she looked back at him with her sweet smile. There wasn't anything about this woman that he would change. He loved her smooth skin, Coke bottle shape, and long hair. Those chubby cheeks and dark eyes. Luciano would never admit it, but what he felt for Tori went beyond infatuation.

"Come take a shower with me before you have to go," she requested, and like always, Luciano followed as if he was under her spell. No man had the power to move him... but Tori Thomas could do so with ease.

The Meeting

LUCIANO DECLINED THE FOOD THAT WAS OFFERED TO him. His meeting with the boss of the Colombian cartel wasn't with the boss at all. Instead, he had Luciano meet with his representative at his restaurant. Luciano understood and respected the fact that Matias kept a low profile.

Only three men were in the room—Luciano, the representative, and a man in the corner wearing a suit. He looked out of place, but Luciano wasn't concerned. The man looked more like an accountant than a cartel member, though bankers and money men were valuable members too.

It took some convincing, but eventually, the representative agreed to hear the Nahtahn Cartel's terms. Miguel agreed that his boss wanted to limit the working parts of his cartel as much as possible. He didn't bother accepting the meeting until Matias heard the Nahtahns had product coming to the States from Cuba and Mexico. And that point, his interest was piqued. When he learned they would deliver the product to his men, already broken down and ready to be distributed, that was all it took for him to agree to a meeting.

"Sebastian," Miguel called, and the man in the suit walked over to the table.

With no words, he lowered himself and snorted the line of cocaine on the table. His head shook and eyes blinked rapidly before he snorted the other two.

"Whew." His body shivered before confusion set in temporarily as he stared at a confident Luciano.

"So?" Miguel said.

"That's some of the purest shit I've ever had. Probably the purest I've ever had. Get it all."

With Sebastian's approval, Miguel stood and extended his hand for Luciano to shake.

"It looks like we have a deal," Miguel said, and Luciano smiled.

"Now that you know the value of our product, let's rework these numbers..."

Later that Afternoon

"Salud!" the brothers yelled on their FaceTime group chat before taking their shots to celebrate Luciano securing the deal.

"Aye, Matias called me raving about the product," Gambino said. "He said it's the purest he's ever gotten, and for the price and ease in which we will deliver, he's glad we let him lock in."

"For him to be saying that knowing who his last supplier was, that means a lot," Gotti said.

"I agree." Luciano chimed in. "The product he was getting from Peru and Amsterdam was insane. I tried the weed from Amsterdam on my last trip here in LA. If we've now exceeded them, we can *easily* bring in more cartels from coast to coast."

"That's what I love to hear," Gambino replied. "How do you feel about traveling for the rest of the year? Maybe the next six months?"

Luciano carefully considered his brother's words. Other than him and Gotti, he didn't have anything to rush back home to. As long as Tori was willing to travel with him and he could bring his personal assistant, Luciano was cool with that.

"Yeah, I'm cool with that. You know I don't really like to talk to people, but I did enjoy securing this deal. As long as I can be back before Rue gives birth, that's fine."

"Yeah, you definitely can't miss that," Gotti agreed.

The trio continued to make their plans, and by the time it was over, Seattle, Miami, Chicago, Minneapolis, Dallas, and Boston were on Luciano's list. After ending the call, he searched the house, not surprised to find Tori in the kitchen.

"I was just about to come get you," she said warmly, setting a steak salad on the island for him.

"Thank you, Tori."

"My pleasure. What do you want for dinner, or were you going out?"

"If I do, will you join me?"

"If you want me to."

"I do, so be ready to go by seven."

"Okay," she agreed with a smile.

"Sit down. There's something I want to discuss with you." Luciano waited until Tori had taken the seat next to him to ask, "How would you feel about traveling with me for the next three to five months? You'll get the same pay, same days off. I'm bringing in my assistant and a security team as well. Everything will be as it is at home... just on the road."

"I would love that. It's not like I have a man or kids or anything, and I can see my family whenever."

"You do have a man," Luciano clarified casually before pouring them both a glass of tequila. He seemed to prefer that when he was in Cali and Mexico these days.

Tori giggled as her head shook. "No I don't. If I did, I wouldn't have fucked you."

"I became your man when you did that lil shit with your tongue under my dick." His head shook as he lifted his glass. "I ain't letting you do that to nobody else."

Tori fell into a fit of laughter, and though he was serious, Luciano smiled.

"Wow, okay. I guess I got a man then." She paused briefly before saying, "If we are going to be together, I can't allow you to pay me to cook for you. It's truly my pleasure."

"Then I'll just give you the money as a monthly allowance. How does that sound?"

"That sounds good," she replied sweetly.

"And you'll be cool with moving into the main house when we get back home?"

"Yes... if that's what you really—"

"I want you," Luciano interrupted her to say. "I've *always* wanted you."

Their eyes remained locked before Tori leaned forward and connected her lips with his.

33

T ori
  One Week Later

"WAIT, WHAT?" LUCIANO ASKED. "YOU WANT ME TO GO to Guadalajara now?"

Tori busied herself on her phone and tried not to eavesdrop. They were about to leave Seattle, and Luciano had secured another cartel. Up until she met the Nahtahn brothers, Tori knew nothing about crime families or drug organizations. At first, she thought they were all about drugs, money, and violence, but the Nahtahns showed her they valued family over everything, and she was proud to be Luciano's woman.

Her eyes scanned the missed calls and text messages from her brother. With a sigh, she stood and hoped she could quickly return his call before the jet took off. There was shuffling in the background and muffled voices before Juan's came through clearly.

"Hello?"

"Hey, you called?"

"Yeah, like a million times. Why didn't you answer?"

"I'm not at home."

Juan sighed. "I need some more money. Can you meet me?"

With a scoff, Tori put her hand on her hip. "I just said I'm not at home, and that's all you call me for now?"

"You mean you're not in Rose Valley Hills?"

Her eyes rolled. "Yes, Juan. That's what I mean."

"Can you call me when you get back?"

"If all you're going to do is ask me for money, no. That hurts my feelings, and it makes me feel like you're using me."

"I'm sorry, baby sis. You're right. That's not my intention. Can you just... call me when you get home so we can talk face to face?"

Tori chewed her cheek as she considered his words. "Yes, that's fine."

"Aight, I love you."

His declaration eased the heaviness on her heart. "I love you too, Juan."

After disconnecting the call, she returned to her seat across from Luciano's. Because her brother had been a sore topic for them in the past, she didn't bother telling him about the call. Luciano saw a side of the drug world that she was unfamiliar with, so Tori understood why he said the things he said about Juan over the years. Regardless, that was her brother, and as much as he frustrated her sometimes, she'd *never* give up on him.

Three Months Later

LUCIANO HAD BEEN A MAN ON A MISSION. HE WAS determined to do what he had to do for the family, but he was also ready to get back home. It tickled Tori when he opted to start spending the weekends back in Rose Valley Hills. While they were there, he was with his family, and she was with hers. For the last six weeks, her brother had been clean, and that was a new record.

While Tori wished it had been his choice, it wasn't. He was arrested for robbery shortly after she talked to him in LA, and because he was a known drug user, he was kept in solitary his entire time there with only an hour of free time outside.

He was currently out on bail and waiting for his trial that would start in three months.

When Tori received a call from an unknown number, she knew it had to be her brother. He'd been out for three days, and she hadn't talked to him since their mother picked him up. Though they had the money for his bail, her mother wanted to let him sit for a while. As much as Tori hated the thought of it, she believed it was for the best, and that was proven to be true. Tori had a surprise for him. She was going to take some of the money she'd saved to get him set up for his new sober life. New phone, car, and apartment. She'd pay up his bills for the first three months and hoped the judge would give him probation only since the store he robbed didn't actually let him take anything before the security guard caught him. He gave the money back before he was sent downtown. All she wanted her brother to do was stay out of trouble and stay clean.

"Hello?" she answered.

"H-hey, sis." At the sound of Juan coughing, she grew concerned.

"Hey, are you okay?"

"Think I'm c-coming down with a c-cold."

Tori's shoulders dropped. She didn't want to believe he was fiending. She didn't want to believe he'd relapsed and was desperate for a hit.

"Well, it is December, so you need to bundle up. It's only going to get colder for the next two months."

"Yeah, you're r-right," Juan said with a laugh before he sniffed. "Listen, Mama said she's cooking dinner for us tonight. You mind picking me up and taking me over there? There's s-something I wanna talk to you about anyway."

Hope filled Tori. If he was using again, he'd be trying to hide. That was a good sign.

"Of course. Just let me know where you'll be, and I'll come pick you up around five."

"Aight, baby sis. S-see you soon."

A smile covered Tori's face as she ended the call. She headed to the kitchen to get started on breakfast for Luciano. His diet was heavy on protein, and he loved a good steak. She decided to make him steak, eggs, and spinach with a side of fruit. As soon as she felt his arms wrap around her from behind, she melted against him.

"Why you get out of bed before I could have you for breakfast?" he asked against her neck before kissing it.

"I know you have a long day, so I wanted to get you fed before you had to leave. You can have me for a late night snack."

"I can't wait that long, baby."

"*Luciano,*" she purred as he slipped his hand under her lace robe and rubbed her ass.

"Hmm?"

Tori moaned when his warm tongue slid from her clit to her asshole. "That feels so good." Luciano spread her cheeks and continued a pleasurable assault on her pussy from behind—sending shivers down her spine every time his tongue circled her back door. He stood and pressed his way inside of her, and she could have cum just off his entrance alone.

His strokes were long, slow, and soft, allowing her to feel literally every inch of him. Her toes curled and body trembled for relief. Every time she was at the edge and about to explode, he'd stop.

"Luciano, please!" she cried, throwing her ass back on him.

"Aight, baby. I'll let you cum."

His strokes picked up pace and hardened, and by the eight one, she was cumming all over him.

"Where you want this shit?" he asked, nearing the edge himself.

"In my pussy. Don't pull out."

Luciano growled and took her hands into his. Pressing her against the counter, he stroked his seeds out until they filled her. After placing kisses on her neck and back, he pulled out. Though she was on birth control, they still took extra precautions. Tori didn't mind having a baby with Luciano eventually, but they were still early in their relationship, and she wanted to be his wife first.

After taking a quick shower where he fucked her against the wall, they returned to the kitchen, and she finished breakfast. Luciano asked about her plans for the day, and she told him, "Family dinner later. I'm gonna pick Juan up around five."

"That's wassup. He still clean?" Luciano checked as he cut into his steak.

"Yes, thankfully."

"Good. I know how important it is for you to have a relationship with him. One where he is healthy."

"Yeah, I think his time away worked wonders. If he can just maintain that same discipline, I think it'll really stick this time."

Luciano grew quiet, which wasn't like him. Usually, their time eating together was their time to talk and bond. It was how they'd gotten to know each other over the years. She decided to wait until they were done eating to ask, "Is something on your mind?"

"There is actually." Luciano stood and tapped the island with the pads of his fingers as he stared at her. "Tomorrow, my brothers are having a little get together. Rue is going to give birth any day now, so we're celebrating up until she does. I want you there... and I want to be able to let them know you're not just my chef anymore. You're my heart."

"Oh." Tori smiled and fanned her face. She wasn't sure what to expect, but she *certainly* wasn't expecting that. "That's... I would love to go. And I don't mind them knowing about us at all. I was wondering when we'd get to the telling our families stage of our relationship."

As Luciano wrapped his arms around her and pulled her close, he assured her, "We're there now."

34

L uciano

THOUGH GOTTI WAS NO LONGER CAPO, HE WANTED TO join Luciano when he went to meet with the leaders of their teams. Quite a few soldiers had been coming up short, and now that Luciano was back home, it was time to handle that. Hampton had taken his cousin's place as capo, and he believed the soldiers were using the transition period to their advantage. For some reason, they thought he wouldn't be as thorough as Gotti. Or maybe they thought he wouldn't find out as quickly. Either way, the excuses and reasons didn't matter. Luciano just needed to make sure the stealing ended.

They stood in the warehouse that was bombed a little over a year ago. It had been completely remodeled and was better than ever. Luciano walked the long line of leaders, looking each one of them in their eyes.

As their team of soldiers stood behind them, Luciano granted Hampton the opportunity to speak to them. They needn't fear *just* the Nahtahn brothers. They needed to fear every member of the family that was in the cartel.

When Luciano grew tired of the talking, he lifted his gun and sent a bullet into the heads of the three leaders whose teams had been coming up short.

"You niggas think you gettin' away with that shit but you ain't," Gotti made clear, lifting his gun and sending bullets into the chests of the soldiers that had been stealing for the leaders.

"Let this be a lesson to you," Hampton said with a grin. "I'm the nice one, but I'll lay a nigga *down* 'bout this money and my respect. Don't make the same mistakes they made. Get the fuck out of here."

The men filed out of the warehouse quickly. While Gotti and Hampton talked, Luciano checked Tori's location. She was supposed to be at her parents' house for dinner, but her phone said she was in the country. He called her, and the phone rang until it went to voicemail. The second time he called, it went straight to voicemail without ringing.

Luciano trusted no man outside of his family, and even some of those were questionable. He for damn sure didn't trust her brother. Tori may have believed her brother was clean, but Luciano's gut was telling him that wasn't the case.

"Some' wrong with my baby," Luciano said absently, heading out of the warehouse.

"Your baby?" Gotti asked.

"Tori."

"Y'all a thing now? That's wassup. Tori thick as *fuck*."

Luciano glared at his brother but didn't bother to address the comment because she was. "I was gon' tell y'all tomorrow. Her location ain't where it should be, and someone just cut her phone off."

"Where was the last ping?"

"In the country."

"Shit. It's the weekend so it's probably packed down there."

Luciano sighed as he hopped into his monster truck. "I know, but you better damn well believe I'm about to find her."

35

Tori

Tori pulled up to the address Juan had given her, and her heart broke a little more. More than anything, she was disappointed in herself. Her intuition told her he'd started using again when she talked to him earlier, but she refused to believe that was the case. As Juan walked out of the crack house, he scratched the back of his neck. One of his hands was stuffed into the pocket of his hoodie as he looked from one side of the street to another.

She quickly locked the doors as her eyes watered. She wanted desperately to believe things could get better for her brother, but each time she had hope in him, he proved that wouldn't be the case. Confusion covered Juan's face when he tried to open the passenger door, but it was locked. He stared at her as she rolled the window down halfway.

"You lied. You're back on that shit, Juan!"

He chuckled as he looked away. "Look, I'm clean, aight? I'ma go to the dinner. I'ma meet you there. I just need a few dollas to pay this man, so he won't kick me out of here. I'm staying here now."

"You're a liar!" she yelled as tears streamed down her face. "I can see it in your eyes, Juan. You're fucking high right now!"

Gritting his teeth, Juan lowered his head as it shook. "I just wanted a lil hit. But I need to pay him, baby sis. I know you got it. Just let me get like fifty dollas. I'on even need that much."

The longer she stared at him, the more her heart broke. Sniffling, Tori started her car as her head shook. "No. I'm not enabling you anymore. If you want to get high, you're going to have to find another way to do it. You're not getting any more money from me."

"You gon' give me some fucking money, Tor." Juan snatched her purse from the passenger seat and ran toward the house.

"Juan!" she yelled, frantically getting out of the car.

As she chased behind him, her heart palpitated. This was the final straw. Regardless of how much she wanted better for her brother, he'd have to want it for himself. She had always been passionate about him getting better, but it didn't matter if the choices he made daily made him worse. So as hard as it was going to be, that day was the day Tori was determined to cut him off.

Tori clawed at his back and reached around him for her purse as he neared the front door of the crack house. She was stunned by the elbow he sent to her face. The force behind it sent her falling into the door.

"Juan?" she called in disbelief.

drove, Luciano held her in the back of the truck. Each time he questioned what made her think he was going to let her leave him, she cried harder. Truth was, Tori didn't want him to, but there was no way in *hell* she'd be able to lie with the man who killed her brother.

36

L uciano

LUCIANO WEIGHED HIS OPTIONS. EVERY BONE IN HIS
body told him that Juan was a cancer that would slowly eat
away at Tori until he killed her. There was no doubt about
that in his mind. For a brief moment, he considered paying
him to leave town, but there was a chance he'd snort the
money up and come begging for more. Though the solution
was clear to Luciano, he wasn't sure he wanted to deal with
the consequences of killing the brother of the woman he'd
fallen in love with.

It took three days to track Juan down. As they sat in
front of the run down shack, Luciano considered what he
wanted to do. Would it matter if he protected Tori if it
caused him to lose her? How would he handle it if he sent
Juan away just for him to come back and attack her again?
Rehab wouldn't work unless Juan was truly dedicated to it.

His mind kept showing him her swollen eye and bruised neck. If it was anyone else, there would be no questions. No inner battle. Her attacker would have already been turned into ashes. With his mind made up about what he was going to do, Luciano got out of the car, and his brothers followed behind.

He kicked the door in and loaded his clip. God forgave, and Tori would have to too. Because there was no way Luciano would allow *anyone* who hurt her to continue to roam this earth. They scanned every room, finding Juan slumped over in the bathroom. As he stared at his lifeless body, Luciano's heart broke for Tori. A part of him thanked God that he didn't have to end Juan's life himself. From the looks of it, he'd stocked up on more crack than he could handle with the money he took from his sister. And the high that he'd been chasing for years finally allowed him to catch it—costing him his life.

One Week Later

THE WEEKEND WAS ONE FILLED WITH CELEBRATING life and death. While Tori and her parents buried her brother, Rue gave birth to a healthy baby girl. Luciano knew the world would be a crazier place now that Gotti Nahtahn had a little girl.

Gambino and Kayla were expecting, but they didn't know if it was a boy or girl yet. Because she'd lost their first baby years ago, Kayla didn't want anyone to know until she made it to her second trimester, but Gambino couldn't resist telling his brothers.

The city was calm and quiet, as if it knew the brothers

needed time. And rest. After the funeral, Luciano left Tori with her parents to go see the newest member of their family.

"You up next," Gotti teased as he held Gabriella.

"Tori talking about we gotta get married first."

"So marry her," Gambino said as Gabriella clutched his finger.

"I will in due time. Maybe in a couple of years."

Both of his brothers looked at him, causing him to chuckle.

"A couple years?" Gambino repeated. "Lu, I can tell you love that woman. The fuck are you waiting for?"

His head shook as he squeezed the back of his neck. "The family comes first. With that, the cartel. It's my priority right now, and I won't marry her until I can give her the priority she deserves."

A hard breath escaped Gotti as he handed Gabriella to Luciano. For a while, none of the brothers spoke as he held the tiny human in his arms. The longer he did, the softer he felt. He smiled as she stared at him with a wonder and innocence Luciano hadn't been privileged to experience before. Not even in his own youth. The world and all of its responsibilities shut off as he held Gabriella, and it was a peace that seemed to have no end.

"Now gimme my baby back and tell me you don't want that."

Before Luciano could respond, his phone vibrated in his pocket. Gambino's did too. Gotti had cut his off. What he wanted didn't matter. The cartel needed him, and he would *always* answer that call.

Luciano ran his fingers through Tori's hair as she lay against his chest. Now that the funeral was over, she'd shut down and didn't want to talk to or be around anyone but him. Luciano was honored to provide a safe space for her, especially since they were at odds before Juan died. He was honest with her about his plans when he found her brother and was grateful he didn't have to take his life. But he would do anything to protect Tori—physically, mentally, and emotionally.

"I remember one night, Juan was so anxious for a hit he climbed out of the bathroom window because we'd barricaded the doors." She laughed sadly then sniffled. "I ran in and tried to stop him, and he kicked me away. I knew at that moment he was willing to do anything to get high, but I never thought he'd really put his hands on me. As sad as I am, a part of me is at peace knowing he's no longer suffering. I probably never would have gotten the healthy version of my brother back, but I wouldn't have been able to live with the last version of him that I encountered either."

Luciano tightened his grip around her and kissed the top of her head.

"Seeing that shit play out in real time makes me want to stop selling that shit, you know? On one hand I can say we aren't responsible for how people consume our stuff. On the other hand, I hate seeing addicts of any kind. I don't think any of my people ever served your brother, but knowing who we are, I can't help but feel some type of responsibility for that."

Tori sighed as she ran her hand up and down his chest. "Some people can smoke it and never become addicted. Some people are consumed by it. It's not your fault. If I blamed or resented you for that, it would just be another way I didn't hold my brother accountable, and I can't do that anymore. Lord knows I love my brother and I'm going to miss him, but I'm also at peace. Does that make me a bad person?"

Luciano tilted her head by her chin so she could look into his eyes. "It doesn't make you a bad person. It makes you human."

Tori found solace in his words, because she kissed him, cuddled against his chest, and finally went to sleep.

Epilogue

G ambino
Some Time Later

PRIDE FILLED GAMBINO AS HIS EYES SCANNED THE room. His wife had given birth to their son—Gambino Junior. Gotti and his family were thriving. He'd proposed recently when they found out Rue was pregnant with their second child. Immediately after the proposal, she tried to beat his ass for thanking him for expanding their chihuahua litter, and it was the funniest thing Gambino had seen. She looked like a little Tasmanian devil as she chased him around the room. As crazy as they were, they balanced each other out, and Gambino was glad there was a woman brave enough to challenge and tame his baby brother.

Luciano had consumed himself with work. So much so that Tori broke up with him. Well, she *thought* she broke up with him. You couldn't really break up with a Nahtahn brother. Regardless of how hard you tried, their love haunted you. And eventually, you found your way back to them.

After securing contracts with all the cartels they wanted to bring into the organization, Luciano decided to take some time off. He couldn't deny how good happiness and having a family of their own looked on his brothers. Surprising them all, he invited Tori to be his date for the Monster's Ball, and she accepted.

Since it was held on New Year's Eve in Miami, Gambino hosted a party for the family at Nahtahn Estate before they were set to leave. The moment was bittersweet. He'd missed the last one, because it was too triggering thinking about his father's heart attack that day, and losing his mother weeks after. It was imperative the Nahtahn family be in attendance that year, and *nothing* was going to stop that.

At the sound of sobs, Gambino shifted his attention toward the fireplace. His eyes watered at the sight of Luciano on bended knee. He didn't believe in ultimatums and was glad Tori hadn't given him one, but he did believe in increasing demand by limiting supply. All it took was a couple of months of not having Tori by his side for Luciano to realize what was truly important, and Gambino couldn't be happier about that.

As they all cheered and celebrated the newly engaged couple, Gambino slipped out of the room. He went to the patio and looked out at the mansions in the cove. His family was happy, healthy, growing, and blessed. They'd taken over coast to coast, and soon would be all over the world. Though Gambino hated the way he came into power, he was determined to take the Nahtahn Cartel to new heights.

The End
Keep Swiping...

Armor and Remedy are coming 3/3.
Join my mailing list or follow me on social media to be
notified of their release.

More Rose Valley Hills:
Sweet
Chapel
Ode to Memphis Series
The Billionaire's Belle
Always the Baker
Mister President
Karrington

More Mafia:

B. Love

Black Mayhem Mafia Saga
The Strongest Whiskee
The Sweetest Knockout
Karrington

Keep Swiping...

B. Love Note

For character visuals:
https://youtu.be/mbEBDm1pyKE

Thank you for reading! I hope you enjoyed my rendition of love in written form. If so, please do me a kindness and leave a review/rating. If you're active on social media, share your thoughts/review there to help spread the word about this book. TikTok girlies, at me. Let's duet ❤

Keep swiping for more of my work, including exclusive eBooks and audiobooks. For event exclusives and projects, check out my website. Follow me on social media if you're there, or sign up for my mailing list for new release information.

Romans 12:18

Mailing list - https://bit.ly/MLBLove22
On all social media - @authorblove

Subscribe to my YouTube channel for book talks, vlogs, and BTS content - https://bit.ly/BLoveYT
For exclusive eBooks, paperbacks, and audiobooks – www.prolificpenpusher.net

We hate errors, but we are human! If the B. Love team leaves any grammatical errors behind, do us a kindness and send them to us directly in an email to emailblove@gmail.com with ERRORS as the subject line.

Follow B. on Amazon for updates on her releases by clicking here.

By the Book with B. Podcast – bit.ly/bythebookwithb

Keep Swiping...

Also by B. Love

Exclusive Audiobooks

The Protectors

In His Possession 2

Rule & Camryn

Power & Elle

Love's Battleground

Love's Garden

In Due Time

Coffee with a Side of You (coming in 2025)

Aspen (coming in 2025)

Karrington (coming in 2025)

Mister Sommelier (coming in 2025)

Mister Chocolatier (coming 3/2025)

Mister Fireman (coming 3/2025)

The Streets Will Never Love Me Like You Do (coming 2025)

Sweet (coming 2025)

Exclusive eBooks

Holly's Jolly Christmas

Who Do You Love?

Hunter and Onyx

Love Me Right Now

She Makes the Dope Boys Go Crazy

Interception

Femi

Audiobooks on Audible/Audiobooks.com/Barnes and Noble/Google Play

Asylum

Merc

The Strongest Whiskee

Her Exception series

Mister Librarian

Mister Jeweler

Mister Concierge

Mister Musician

Mister Teacher

Mister Artist (coming 2/2025)

Mister President (coming 2/2025)

Always the Baker (coming 2025)

Chapel

Banking on Love series

Ode to Memphis books 1, 3, and 4

The Billionaire's Belle

The Sweetest Knockout

Black Mayhem Mafia books 1-5

Also by B. Love

Standalone Romance

Love Me Until I Love Myself (Christian Romance)

Give Me Something I Can Feel

Saving All My Love for You

To Take: A Novella

In Haven

Weak: An Irresistible Love

The Ashes: The Medina Sisters' Story

Just Say You Love Me

If You Ever Change Your Mind #1

Coffee with a Side of You #1

If He Loves Me #1

In Due Time #1

Will You Still Want Me? #1

If You'll Let Me

Til Morning #1

I'll Be Bad For You #1

Just Love Me (Shenaé Hailey)

Due for Love (Shenaé Hailey)

Til I Overflow

Flesh, Flaws, and All (Christian romance)

Make it Last

Straddling His Soul #1

Fingers on his Soul

My Love Wasn't Meant for You

The Preying Pastor

Everything I Desire

Someone She Loved #1

Give Me Love

Love Me for Christmas

Trapped Wishes #1

Yours to Have #1

Unequivocally, Blindly, Yours

Brief Intermission

But Without Haste #1

Last Chance to Love #1

Strumming My Pain #1

With His Song #1

Held Captive by a Criminals Heart #1

Fans Only

To Protect & Swerve

Now Playing: Reel Love

Faded Love

Just Like I Want You

Lie in It

April's Showers

The Mourning Doves

Finding a Wife for My Husband

In The Lonely Hour

Ours for Hours

Loving the Lonely

A Valentine for Christmas

The Love Dealer

The Love List

Santa's Cummin' to Town #1

Holly's Jolly Christmas

Bloody Fairy

Who Do You Love?

His Sleeping Beauty #1

The Billionaire's Belle

Dali

The Deed to a Gangsta's Heart

The Protectors

Asylum #1

Merc #1

The Protectors #1

The Strongest Whiskee

Aspen #1

Karrington

The Boss Babe Series

Tampering with Temptation

Hungry for Her

Seducing a Savage

The Office Series

Her Exception 1: An Enemies to Lovers Romance

Her Exception 2: A Friends to Lovers Romance

Her Exception 3: A Fake Relationship Romance

The Hibiscus Hills Standalone Series

A Picture Perfect Love

The Mister Series

Mister Librarian #1

Mister: The Mister Series Prelude

Mister Jeweler #1

Mister Concierge #1

Mister Musician #1

Mister Teacher #1

Mister 2

Mister Sommelier

Mister Chocolatier #1

Mister Fireman

Mister 3

Mister Artist

Mister President #1

Banking on Love Series

60 Days to Love

The Business of Lust

Majority Rules #1

Romance Series

Love Me Right Now (1-2) #1

(Website Exclusive)

To Take: Crimson Trails series (1-5)

Send me (part 1) I'll go (part 2) #1

*The Love Series – The Love We Seek, The Love We Find, The Love We Share

Harts Fall Series – With All My Heart, With All My Trust, With All My Love (Shenaé Hailey)

Her Unfaithful Husband, His Loyal Wife, Their Impenetrable Bond (Shenaé Hailey)

Love is the Byline

Love's battleground

Love's garden #1

Ode to Memphis

Love Letters from Memphis

The Streets Will Never Love Me Like You Do

A Memphis Gangsta's Pain

In the Heart of Memphis

Rose Valley Hills

Sweet

Chapel

Ode to Memphis Series

The Billionaire's Belle

Always the Baker

Karrington

Mister President

Jasper Lane

Steeped in his Love

Dali

The Deed to a Gangsta's Heart

Standalone Urban

To Be Loved by You

His Piece of Peace #1

Her Piece of Peace

Her piece of peace: The Wedding

Hunter and Onyx: An Unconventional Love Story

Thief #1

A Hustler's Heaven in Hiding

His thug love got me weak

If I Was Ya Man

A Gangsta's Paradise #1

LoveShed

Kisses for my Side Mistress

Set Up for Love

Promise to Keep it Trill

Her Heart, His Hood Armor

Her Gangster, The Gentleman

Her Only Choyce

Let it H*E (Constance)

Yours to Keep

A Thug in Need of Love

The Sweetest Knockout Standalone Series

The Sweetest Knockout

Black Mayhem Mafia Family Saga

In His Possession

Her Deep Reverence

A Heart's Rejection

Under His Protection #1

A Father's Objection

In His Possession 2

A Heart's Connection

Indiscretion #1

Succession #1

Resurrection #1

Interception

Gucci Gang Saga

I Need A Gangsta

One Love

Urban Series

She Makes the Dopeboys go Crazy (1-2)

Caged Love: A Story of Love and Loyalty (1-5)

If You Give Me Yours (part 1) I'll Give You Mine (part 2) #1

Loved by a Memphis Hoodlum 3

It Was Always You 2

The Bad Boy I Love 2

No Love in His Heart 3

My Savage and His Side Chick 2

So Deep In Love

Faded Mirrors

Behind Every Great Gangsta

(Coming to Amazon 3/7/25)

Beginning Career Titles

*(Series are separated. Characters are overlapped. These titles do not have to be read together, but if you'd prefer to know what stories everyone is from, you can read them in this order. **Power and Elle and Rule and Camryn can be read alone without reading anything else**.)*

Kailani and Bishop: A Case of the Exes 1-3

Alayziah: When Loving him is Complicated 1-2

Teach Me how to Love Again 1-2

—

Power and Elle: A Memphis Love Story

Rule and Camryn 1-4: A Memphis Love Story

Femi

—

Young Love in Memphis 1-3

But You Deserve Better

Traditionally Published

The Loyal Wife

End.